BREAKFAST AT SADIE'S

Also by Lee Weatherly:

CHILD X
MISSING ABBY

BREAKFAST AT SADIE'S

Lee Weatherly

David Fickling Books

OXFORD · NEW YORK

BREAKFAST AT SADIE'S
A DAVID FICKLING BOOK 0 385 60779 2

Published in Great Britain by David Fickling Books,
a division of Random House Children's Books

This edition published 2005

1 3 5 7 9 10 8 6 4 2

Typeset in New Baskerville by Palimpsest Book Production Limited,
Polmont, Stirlingshire

DAVID FICKLING BOOKS
31 Beaumont Street, Oxford, OX1 2NP, UK
A division of RANDOM HOUSE CHILDREN'S BOOKS
61–63 Uxbridge Road, London W5 5SA
A division of The Random House Group Ltd

RANDOM HOUSE AUSTRALIA (PTY) LTD
20 Alfred Street, Milsons Point, Sydney,
New South Wales 2061, Australia

RANDOM HOUSE NEW ZEALAND LTD
18 Poland Road, Glenfield, Auckland 10, New Zealand

RANDOM HOUSE (PTY) LTD
Endulini, 5A Jubilee Road, Parktown 2193, South Africa

THE RANDOM HOUSE GROUP Limited Reg. No. 954009
www.**kids**at**randomhouse**.co.uk

A CIP catalogue record for this book is available from the British Library

Printed and bound in Great Britain by
Clays Ltd, St Ives plc

Acknowledgements

Thanks are due to Annick and Bob Hammersley of the Anchorage Guest House, Brixham, who gave me an inside glimpse of the workings of the B&B world, and answered many nosy questions;

To Dr Nick Lewis, who suggested Guillain-Barré Syndrome;

And to my husband, for reading every draft, listening patiently to endless writer-angst, and offering calm, constant support. I couldn't do it without you.

For my mother,
who read Shakespeare to me as bedtime
stories and fished my own early story
attempts out of the bin,

and Moise,
who, years later, reads his honorary
daughter's stories with such pride.

With much love to you both.

Lazy Crazy

'It's just not good enough, Sadie; you need to apply yourself more.' Mum frowned as she worked our industrial iron, pressing the creases out of a sheet. The smell of warm cotton filled the room. 'It's like you don't even try.'

Thanks so much for that insight, Mum. I took the sheet from her as she pulled it out, and started folding. The hot linen baked my arms.

'Sadie, answer me!' *Hiss, hiss.* Steam rose up, flushing her face and curling her short brown hair.

'I do try,' I said in a monotone.

'Well, you could certainly fool me.' Mum yanked a bit of duvet cover taut as she closed the iron. Her hand slipped as she was doing it, so that when she opened the iron again there was a massive crease. She huffed out a sigh, and grabbed the spray-bottle of water.

'Three out of ten! Sadie, honestly, that's just being lazy. You can do better than that.'

Leave me alone! How would *you* know? But I knew

better than to say that. I laid the freshly folded sheet on top of the rest. In the corner of our lounge, the TV was on – one of those brainy quiz shows that people go on to show off how clever they are. *Ooh yes, I believe the answer would be the central Amazon basin, Madam.*

Mum went on for ages as she opened and shut the iron. What about my future? What about university? My life would be ruined if I didn't start pulling my socks up. I kept folding sheets and duvet covers like a robot as the words pounded against my skull.

Finally she switched the iron off. 'Sadie, I know you think I'm just nagging at you, love, but you really need to apply yourself more. You're a bright girl; you need to start acting like it.'

She went into the kitchen to start making tea, and I bolted off to my room, banging the door as hard as I dared. God, she never stopped! She'd go on about my marks if we were crossing the North Pole on dogsleds.

I threw myself on my bed, trying to ignore the pile of books and papers that crouched on my desk like tarantulas. Yes, right, I just needed to apply myself more. How silly of me not to have figured it out before.

I heard my Aunt Leona come in, and then a few minutes later the sound of her and Mum talking in the kitchen. I rolled my eyes. Trust her to get out of helping with the ironing. Aunt Leona kept well away from anything resembling work when she stayed with us at our B&B, which thankfully wasn't that often. She thought Brixham was a tourist trap, and only came here when she wanted to do a flounce on her latest boyfriend.

I rolled over on my back, staring at the ceiling. If I strained my ears, I could just hear the sound of the ocean across the street, whispering against the beach. My room faced out to the side of the house, so I couldn't actually see the water from my window. But when my window was open, like now, I could smell the sea air, and hear the seagulls shrieking to each other. They congregated on top of our house sometimes as if they were having a convention.

Everyone thought Mum was mad to have kept going with Grace's Place after my dad died. But one thing you can say about Mum, she doesn't give up easily – whether it's running a massive bed and breakfast on her own, or deciding that I'm some sort of genius who should be getting brilliant marks.

Taking out my mobile phone, I started to text my friend Tara. She wasn't my best friend, just a friend. My best friend was Kate, but she was gone – she and her family moved to Australia last summer. We had emailed for a few months after she left, but it just wasn't the same. We hadn't written to each other in ages now.

I looked down at the little plastic screen, and my fingers hesitated over the keys. To be honest, I really didn't feel like a *hi, how r u, what r u watching on telly* conversation just then. I glanced at my schoolbooks again, waiting on the desk.

Could I do better, if I tried? I bit my lip, thinking about it.

OK, completely mad idea . . . but what if I wasn't

thick? What if I just needed to try harder? My heart quickened as I stared at my books. Maybe . . . maybe Mum was right, and I was just lazy. Maybe what I *thought* was trying wasn't actually putting any effort in at all. So if I really, really worked at it, harder than I had ever worked before . . .

Slowly, I clicked the phone shut and got up, opening my maths book. A drawing of a square inside a circle looked up at me. *The square has sides of 2.83 centimetres each. Calculate the circle's area.*

I took a deep breath and sat down at my desk.

Chicken Scratchings

'Sadie, you're not listening!' Hannah nudged my arm. The canteen throbbed with shouts and conversations, and the smell of greasy chips hung in the air.

'Hang on.' I tapped the numbers into my calculator again, and the answer came out the same – nine point two centimetres. Yes! Bubbles of excitement popped in my stomach. On to number six.

Hannah shook her head and turned back to Alice. 'Anyway, as I was saying . . . to my friends who actually *listen* to me . . .'

I had worked on my maths homework until almost midnight the night before, going over and over it. After a few hours I started to feel like maybe I was understanding it a bit. In fact . . . looking it over now, it seemed pretty much perfect.

Beside me, Tara slid a paper across to Hannah. 'Oi, I can't read your writing. Is that a nine or a seven?'

Hannah broke off, and rolled her eyes. 'Try learning your numbers, you thickie. It's a nine. You know, nine – it comes after eight.'

'Ta, my dear.' Tara was already busy copying down the next problem. Hannah never bothered her, no matter how sarky she got. The two of them had been best mates since primary, and Tara had skin as thick as a rhino's anyway.

Hannah looked at me again. 'Ooh, look at you, Miss Swot all of a sudden.'

'Just checking my handwriting.' I put my calculator away and made my voice gravel. '*Neatness is important, people! I shan't strain my eyes to make out chicken scratchings, I shall just throw them in the bin!*'

Hannah burst out laughing, even though she's heard me imitate the Battleship a hundred times. 'Sadie, you sound just like her! That's too scary.' She glanced at my paper. 'Do you want to check it against mine?'

I grinned at her, thinking, *Hannah, you are going to be soo surprised.* 'No, that's OK.'

She raised her feathery brown eyebrows. 'You sure? You could get a good mark for a change.'

Oh, thanks. I felt like telling her off, but instead I pursed my mouth up like a toddler, and gave her a big-eyed look. 'Ooh, but me wouldn't know what to do with a big mark. Me can only count up to five so far.'

'Really? That high?' Hannah laughed and turned back to Alice, leaning on her elbow as the two of them chatted. I shoved away my irritation, and looked over my homework again.

It still seemed perfect. A perfect paper. I was actually looking forward to maths for a change.

Perfect Perky Swans

Except wouldn't you know it, the Battleship chose *that* day to be off ill, and of course the supply teacher didn't have a clue and just gave us a study hour. Which meant that everyone passed notes and talked, and my maths homework stayed in my folder.

Never mind, I told myself. *Monday. They'll see on Monday.*

After school, I went straight home as usual to help out with our B&B, even though most people, ones who had a life, actually got to do something interesting instead. I threatened once to report Mum to the authorities for child labour, but she just pulled a sour face and said that a nice restful spell in prison would be a holiday compared to her usual existence.

I moved around the dining room, making up the place settings. A pile of fresh serviettes was slung over my arm, and a basket of silverware rattled at my side. I worked more slowly than usual, lost in a lovely warm daydream. Sadie, the one everyone turned to for help with their homework. The one no one laughed at in class any more, because she always got the right answers. I smiled to myself as I placed forks and knives on the tables.

Our dining room has eight round tables, one for each of the guest bedrooms upstairs. Each table has a frilly white cloth, and a little vase with fresh flowers in it. The ceiling's painted pale blue, to match the view of the ocean outside. That was my dad's idea.

Swipe the mat clean – the special ones that Mum bought, with the picture of Old Brixham on them – then fold the serviette in the swan shape that Dad liked so much. Fork, knife, spoon. Make sure they're gleaming.

It was really no surprise that I didn't have a life outside school. Especially once Kate moved away, abandoning me to the serviettes. She used to help me with the dining room, and we'd have a laugh doing it. Wars with the serviette swans, pecking each other with their cloth bills. Now it was just me, and you couldn't do that on your own without being very sad.

'Oh, he just won't stop!' Aunt Leona appeared in the doorway, waving her mobile. 'Listen to this: *Where are you? Have you broken up with me? What about our holiday? Desperate to hear your voice!*' She groaned and threw the phone onto the sideboard. It clinked against the clean coffee cups.

'*As if* I'd feel like going to the Canaries with him now – I just want to be left alone!'

'So don't go.' I rubbed a bit of jam off a salt cellar with my cloth.

'Well, I don't plan to! That's what I'm doing *here*.'

'Well, good. So . . . no problem, right?' I moved on to the next table, swiping the mats clean.

Aunt Leona glared at me and went over to the bay window, leaning a bony hip against the sill and looking pointedly out at the ocean. She hated it when you told her there was no problem. She loved problems, so long as she got to star in them.

Aunt Leona was Mum's younger sister. *Much* younger; she was only twenty-one. You could still tell they were sisters, though. She had the same narrow face and wavy brown hair as Mum, except that hers reached down to her waist, and she sometimes wore loads of little plaits through it. Mum always wore her hair too short, and it stuck up all over the place. She'd spend ages going at it with a wet brush and a hairdryer, only for it to start sticking up again about an hour later.

I don't look like either of them. I'm tall and blonde, like my dad was. He used to call me his farm girl. I guess he meant that I looked like I should be outdoors, or something. Hopefully he didn't mean that I actually looked like I should be out milking the cows. On the other hand, Kate said once that I looked like a Swedish tennis player, which is far cooler than the farm girl thing.

'Though three weeks in the Canaries would still be better than *here*, even with Ron the Loser,' continued Aunt Leona, scowling out the window. 'It's July! Where's the sun?'

8

I folded a serviette. 'Do you fancy helping me with this, to take your mind off it?'

She gave me a look. 'No, not really. I'm meant to be on holiday, aren't I?'

'Yes, but there's only a few tables left. Then after that, you could help me with the laundry.' I said it really innocently, like she might actually say, *Wow, what a great idea! Let me at that laundry, I can hardly wait!*

She sniffed, and pushed herself up from the windowsill. 'I'm going for a walk to clear my head a bit. It's very stressful, you know, all this with Ron – you wouldn't understand, you're too young.'

And off she went, in a swirl of brown hair. I finished up the tables and dumped the silverware basket on the sideboard. It was a massive antique one, with scrollwork on the sides, and lots of little niches and drawers. Dad bought it at auction for practically nothing, and then spent almost a year sanding it down and fixing it up in his spare time.

I glanced around the room, making sure that it looked OK, or else I'd have Mum jumping all over me. Were the white tablecloths straight? The serviette swans all standing to attention? The silverware so gleaming that you could see yourself upside down in the spoons?

Yes, it was all fine. Perfect perky swans. And now on to my other fun chores.

But for a moment I just stood there, leaning against the sideboard and looking out of the window. You could see right across the broad curve of the bay, clear to the other side of Brixham, where pastel houses climbed up the hill. When the sun was shining, there was sometimes a reflection of the water dancing on the ceiling, like wavery diamonds. It was probably fun to eat in here, like being on a boat.

The dining room was only for our guests, though. Mum and I ate in our flat, which looked out to the car park.

It's Just Carelessness

The faint sound of splintering glass shattered through the air, bringing me back to planet earth. 'Oh, *damn*,' said Mum's voice.

I shoved the spare serviettes in a drawer in the sideboard and went down the corridor, pushing open the swinging door that lead to our flat. There were no antiques in here; it was all seventies swirling carpet and faded furniture. I found Mum in the kitchen, squatting on the floor with the dustpan and brush.

'Don't come in, there's glass everywhere,' she snapped when she saw me.

'What happened?' I propped a shoulder against the doorpost.

'Oh, I don't know . . . I was putting the dishes away, and a glass just slipped out of my hand, somehow.' Her face wore a tight scowl as she dumped tinkling shards of glass into the bin. 'That's the third one this week; I must be going senile.'

Glancing over at our dining table I saw that she had her ledger out, and bank statements spread across everything. She did her accounts once a month, and it put her in a bad mood for days.

Mum sighed as she stood up. 'I desperately need a cup of tea. How about you?'

If I'd said no, I'd have had to start folding sheets and doing the ironing. I nodded, and Mum filled two mugs with steaming water from our industrial water heater. It was hooked up to the boiler, so there was hot water all the time.

'There, that's better.' Mum sat down at the dining table, pushing the pile of bank statements aside. She glanced up at me. 'Did Leona help you with the dining room?'

Was she serious? I shook my head, blowing on my tea. 'No. Why would she do that?'

'Well, she said she was going to.'

'What, to get out of helping with the dishes?'

Mum frowned, but couldn't actually deny it. 'Well, she's having a hard time at the moment; all this stuff with Ron . . .'

I shrugged. When was Aunt Leona *not* having a hard time? But I didn't say it. Mum had a blind spot the size of an ocean liner about Aunt Leona. At least she lived in London, and only graced us with her presence a couple of times a year.

'Anyway, how did you do in school today?' asked

Mum, shoving her short brown hair back. It stuck up like an owl's tufts.

My stomach turned into a fist. 'Oh . . . OK.'

'How did you do in English? You had an essay due back, right?'

'Um – well, I got a D on it. But Mum, listen, I'm waiting to get my maths homework back, and—'

She blew out a breath. 'Oh, *Sadie* . . . a D? That's almost failing!'

'Yes, but – Mum, listen—'

'You *must* start applying yourself more. It's just like with the SATs, you went in there and obviously didn't even try!'

I stared down at my tea. I had been dreading the SATs all year. I had *known* that I'd be rubbish at them; my brain turns into a freezing ball of ice whenever I sit exams.

Mum pounded a pile of bank statements together, banging them against the table. 'You've got to stop being lazy, Sadie.'

I clenched the warm mug. 'But I think I'll do really well on my maths homework! Mum, wait and see, I'll get it back on Monday and I can show you—'

She stood up and put her ledger away, creaking the desk drawer shut. 'Well, I should hope so. Because there's no excuse. It's just carelessness.'

Carelessness. I couldn't say anything. Mum sighed, and lifted her teacup. 'Sadie, I don't mean to get at you, but you just don't seem to understand how important school is—'

And suddenly her hand trembled, and there was tea everywhere.

'Oh!' Mum jumped back. Her teacup lay on the floor. Tea had splattered all over her legs, staining her beige trousers. 'Oh, I can't believe I've done it *again*!'

'It's just *carelessness*, that's all.' My voice shook. I slammed out of the room. Forget the laundry. Forget everything. Nothing I ever did was right anyway.

Mucking It Up

Mrs Shipton was back on Monday, sniffling slightly but as charming as ever. She was old, massive and grey, so of course she was called the Battleship. It was such a perfect nickname for her that I bet even her husband secretly called her that.

She clapped her hands. 'Right, everyone! Give your homework papers to a neighbour to mark, and we'll go through the answers.'

She always did this, and I hated it. I didn't like anyone else to see what awful marks I got. They always did, of course, and then Hannah or Tara would say something like, *Hurrah, Sadie, another brilliant paper!* They weren't even trying to be nasty, which almost made it worse.

Anyway, we did a three-way swap, and I handed my paper to Tara with a grin. It felt like Christmas morning. I'd go home this afternoon and tell Mum how well I had done, and she'd be gobsmacked. I pictured her brown eyes shining as she said, *Sadie, you've done such a good job! I'm so proud of you!*

The Battleship went through the problems, squeaking the answers onto the whiteboard as she explained about the Pythagorean theorem and how to find the area of a circle. Hannah got eight out of ten. One of the ones she missed was easy.

'Papers back to their owners, please.' The Battleship clicked over to her desk, her shiny black shoes clutching her ankles like they were strangling them.

I handed Hannah her paper back. 'Here you go. You only missed two.'

'Here's yours, Sadie.' Tara pushed my paper across to me, and my breath stopped. She had slashed big blue X's all over it. *Five out of ten.*

'You've marked my paper wrong,' I hissed.

Her red eyebrows shot up. 'I have not.'

'But I did better than this!'

'No, you didn't.'

I grabbed her paper from her and started comparing the answers. Meanwhile the Battleship was honing right towards us, like we were caught in her deadly radar. 'What's the problem, you girls?'

My face burned. 'Nothing – just – I think Tara marked my paper wrong.'

The Battleship picked my paper up, her squinty grey eyes flicking over it.

'You're right,' she said.

'See!' I said to Tara. I don't usually gloat, but I

couldn't help it. I had worked so hard, and I *knew* she had mucked it all up.

The Battleship picked up a pen from our table and changed something on my paper. She dropped it in front of me. 'You got number three wrong, too.'

Ice froze in my veins as I stared down at the *4/10* she had scrawled across the top of the paper. Four out of ten. As awful as ever. All that work, and it hadn't made any difference at all. I heard a snicker run across the room, and I cringed.

The Battleship heaved out a breath. 'Sadie, really, you must start spending more time on your work. This is abysmal.' She lumbered back up to the front of the room.

I forced out a laugh, flopping back in my seat with a smirk so that everyone could see that I wasn't bothered in the least. (I wasn't about to ask her what *abysmal* meant. I could guess.)

'Don't mind her, she's an old cow,' whispered Hannah.

'Oh, I don't care; I was only winding her up,' I muttered back. 'I mean, come on – *me* worrying about my marks?' I rolled my eyes.

Tara laughed. 'Yeah, it's not like you're used to getting anything higher.'

'Not our Sadie,' said Hannah. She patted me on the head.

'It's a blonde thing.' I put my finger on my cheek, simpering, and they both cracked up, spluttering behind their hands.

Neither of them noticed that I wasn't laughing. Kate would have, but Kate was ten thousand miles away in Australia, which was no help at all.

'Quiet, you girls!' barked the Battleship, banging her hand on her desk. 'It's not a laughing matter.' She stopped, and her mouth creaked into a smile.

'Milly, how did *you* do?'

Hannah stuck her finger down her throat. You could just feel the hatred in the room as everyone glared at Milly.

She had been looking out of the window when the Battleship called on her, playing with her thick black hair. Now she looked up with this perfect *pretend* surprise. As though the Battleship didn't always want to parade her about in front of the rest of us.

'Ten out of ten, miss.' She sounded bored.

'Good girl. Collect the papers for me, will you?'

Milly stood up with a sigh and started taking the papers up. She'd probably get totally flattened by one of the ruling cliques if she didn't have this air of complete assurance about her. No one was really sure what she might do, I guess, so she was pretty much left alone.

I handed her my homework without looking at her. It wasn't fair. Milly didn't even seem to care that she could turn out perfect papers. She could probably turn them out in her sleep.

I couldn't get anything right even when I tried.

It's a Blonde Thing

The sun came out for a change that afternoon, so a big group of us went outside after lunch, basking in a sunny corner of the courtyard. Hannah and Tara sat together, of course; so did Jan and Alice. Best friends everywhere you looked. It was enough to make you sick, if you were the jealous type. Good thing I wasn't, huh?

'Sadie, tell them how you had the Battleship going this morning.' Hannah nudged me, and grinned at the others. 'It was *so* funny. She came steaming over . . .'

So I had to go through it all again, imitating the Battleship's gravelly voice. Everyone hooted when I said, *It's a blonde thing*. Tara was actually lying on the ground, gasping and stomping her feet on the tarmac. 'Oh, that was so brilliant! Oh, I'm going to wet myself . . .'

My smile was pasted on my face. It would shatter in a million pieces if I hung about here any longer. I stood up. 'Right, the blonde's going to the loo now.'

'If she can find it!' Hannah spluttered. Everyone fell about with hysteria, clutching each other's arms. I laughed too, and made my *simper, simper* face.

Once I was out of sight around the corner of the building, I pressed myself against the rough bark of the oak tree that grows beside the art block, and switched on my mobile. You're not supposed to take them to school, but everyone does.

17

'Good afternoon, Drake Secondary School.'

I cupped my hand around the phone, praying they wouldn't hear the shouts from a bunch of Year Sevens who were kicking a ball around. 'Yes, hello, this is Celia Pollock, Sadie's mum. She's in Year Nine.'

'Oh, hello, Mrs Pollock.'

My heart was jack-knifing against my ribs, but my voice came out calmly. 'I'm sorry, but I forgot to let you know that Sadie has a dentist's appointment this afternoon. I'm on my way to get her now.'

A rustle of papers from down the phone. 'Oh, I see. Yes, I'll let her teachers know.'

'Thanks.' I hung up, and let out a breath.

It's dead easy to sound like Mum – I just lower my voice a few notches and *think serious*. I don't do it often, though. I save it for emergencies, when I really need to get away from school.

This was *so* one of those times. If I stayed I'd either burst into tears or strangle someone.

I didn't go back to the group. I hid out in the loo until the bell rang, and then I grabbed my things and jogged through the corridors, weaving through the blue uniforms.

'My mum's waiting outside,' I called to Mrs Clark, the receptionist.

'She needs to sign you out,' she shouted after me, but I was already out the front door.

Twenty Per Cent of B&Bs

Breakwater Beach was dead small, and had pebbles instead of sand, but I loved it there. It was only just across the street from our house, but it was down a hill, so I knew Mum wouldn't spot me. Dad used to take me there when I was little. We'd have picnics with Ribena and chocolate biscuits, and he'd show me how to skim rocks across the water.

Now I stood on the beach and skimmed rocks for ages, until my uniform felt clammy from the sea air. After a while it was time to go home, but I still stayed there, throwing pebble after pebble, watching them splash. Anything was better than going into the house and having Mum ask how I did in school. Anything. An attack of killer jellyfish. Being dragged under by a sea monster.

'Hi,' said a voice at my elbow. I looked down and saw Marcus, the weedy little dweeb who lived next door. It was just as well that his mum taught him at home, because he would have no friends at all at school. It would be like throwing a sirloin steak into a cage of starving lions.

'Hi,' I said back, not really looking at him.

He shoved his glasses up his nose, squinting in the salty air. 'What are you doing?'

Scuba diving, can't you tell? I threw the rest of the

pebbles I was holding into the bay all at once. They landed with little gulps, like fish bobbing up. Grabbing my bag, I started to climb up the rise towards the road.

'Sadie, wait! Are you leaving?'

How could he be so clever when all he ever did was ask stupid questions? I turned round, my foot slipping slightly on the damp rocks. 'Yes, Marcus, I'm leaving now.'

'Hang on, I want to ask you something.'

'What? What could you possibly want to ask me?'

He blinked, his eyes looking enormous behind his round glasses. 'Mum wants me to do a project for school, and I thought I'd do something on business. Like, how to run a business more efficiently. So I thought I could help out with your mum's B&B, and do a report on it.'

'Well, you'll have to ask Mum, it's nothing to do with me.'

He scrambled up the slope, and stood there with me while I waited to cross the road. Across the street, our house rose up on a slight hill – a rambling old Victorian, painted white. Marcus squinted at it.

'See, Mum said that your B&B isn't as busy as some of the others in town, so I thought it would be an ideal business to study, because you're probably doing loads of things wrong – I mean, you're a waterfront property, so you should, in theory, be successful. Though *having said that*, did you know that over twenty per cent of B&Bs in this country go bankrupt within ten years?'

I looked at him as the cars whizzed past. He straightened his glasses. 'I've been doing research.'

'Well, cheers for that, Marcus.' A gap came in the traffic, and I plunged across the street, with Marcus right on my heels. He followed me up to the house, still talking as we passed the green and white sign that Dad had painted: *Grace's Place, Bed and Breakfast.* Grace was my grandmother. When my dad converted the house to a B&B, he named it after her.

'So I want to do a thorough business analysis of where you're going wrong, and I also thought I could do a report on what sort of clients stay at B&Bs in Brixham, contrasting it with—'

As I opened the front door, my elbow practically bopped Marcus on the nose, he was standing so close.

'*Mar*-cus—'

'What? Anyway, I need to talk to your mum about my project.' He shoved into the house ahead of me.

I groaned and followed him into the front hallway. I had just put my bag down when I heard Aunt Leona's voice coming from our sitting room, sounding high-pitched and strange. 'Celia! Can't you get up? My God, what's wrong?'

And Mum's voice, wavering all over the place as she said, 'I don't know – it's my legs—'

'Marcus, you have to leave,' I hissed.

'But—'

'*Now!*' I pushed him out the door, banging it shut behind me, and ran into the sitting room.

Travelling in Style

Mum sat slumped on the floor, her back against the coffee table, her face as white as a clown's. Aunt Leona hovered at her side, pulling at her arm. 'Come on, let's get you up – you can do it, you've just had a bit of a funny turn, that's all—'

'Sadie!' gasped Mum when she saw me.

'Mum, what's wrong?' It felt like my heart was trying to claw its way out of my chest.

'I don't know, it's my legs. They just – seem to have stopped working—' She tried to laugh, but didn't do a very good job of it. I grabbed her other arm, and Aunt Leona and I struggled her up to her feet. But she couldn't stand once we got her there. She fell against Aunt Leona's side, and the three of us almost went crashing down.

'No, I'm sorry, it's no good—' We got her into the armchair, and she gripped the cushion, her nails digging into it. 'This is so strange; I don't know what's wrong with me . . .'

Aunt Leona licked her lips. 'Well . . . maybe if you rest for a bit? It can't be anything serious; you were fine just a few seconds ago!' Her voice rose, cracking as it went.

'I— I don't know,' said Mum. 'I don't know.'

The room felt too small. My heart smashed against

my ribs, over and over, like a sledgehammer.

Aunt Leona hugged herself. 'Well, maybe if—'

'I'm calling an ambulance,' I blurted out, and before anyone could argue with me, I grabbed up the phone and jabbed in 999. My throat was so clenched I could hardly breathe, but somehow I managed to tell them my name, and what was wrong. Mum stared at me as I spoke, her eyes huge.

Ten minutes later, flashing red lights pulsed in our window, and the ambulance arrived. I ran to the front door, and two men in green jumpsuits came in, going straight to the lounge as if they had rehearsed it. They leaned over Mum, checking her pulse and asking questions. It didn't take them any time at all to decide that she should go to hospital.

'Oh my God, is she all right?' Aunt Leona clutched my arm as they gently lifted Mum onto a stretcher. 'Is she going to be OK?'

'I'm sure she'll be fine, love,' said one of the paramedics. He patted Mum on the shoulder, smiling at her. Mum tried to smile back, but I could tell how scared she was. She looked tiny as they strapped her onto the stretcher, like a little girl in a horror film.

Aunt Leona put her arms around me and started to cry, pressing her head against mine and practically smothering me with all her hair. 'Oh, this is so terrible . . . I just can't bear this . . .'

'Leona, please,' said Mum weakly.

I pulled her arms off me. She was like an octopus. 'Aunt Leona, it's OK. It's OK, really.' Obviously it wasn't, but I thought I'd throttle her if she didn't shut up.

'Who's riding in the ambulance, then?' asked the other paramedic.

'Me,' I said quickly, before Aunt Leona could open her mouth. She looked at me, her brown eyes damp and wounded. 'You follow in the car,' I told her. 'Because I can't drive, see?'

Her mouth tucked in a bit, but she nodded. 'Yes, all right. Fine.'

The paramedics carried Mum slowly out of the front door, careful not to bang the stretcher against the doorpost. I felt insubstantial, like a ghost drifting after them, and at the same time everything was hyper-real, magnified a hundred times. A blue Toyota slowed down as it passed us. A man walking an Alsatian stopped across the street, staring. I hugged myself and looked away.

They loaded Mum into the back of the ambulance, sliding her in like something on an assembly line. 'Right, love, you can hop in,' said one of them to me. He was balding, with short black hair and friendly eyes.

He held a hand out to me, taking my arm as I climbed into the back of the ambulance. 'You can sit here,' he said, showing me a little seat on the floor. It was just like you see in films, with complicated-looking machines everywhere.

Mum lay on her stretcher, trying to smile. 'Travelling in style, aren't we?'

I lifted my lips to smile back, but didn't quite manage it. My pulse pounded in my ears. Oh, God, it was just like when Dad collapsed that final time.

I was only nine when it happened. He was in the lounge, just a few feet from where Mum had fallen. I held onto his hand, and thought I was going to faint when the paramedics came for him. Mum rode with him; they wouldn't let me. The doors of the ambulance closed behind him and I couldn't stop crying. It was like they were swallowing him up. And actually they were, because then he went into hospital and never left it again.

And now it was Mum inside the ambulance, swallowed up with me.

The other paramedic hopped into the front and we lurched off, crunching away down our gravel drive. I held onto the sides of my tiny seat, and thought, *Oh, please God, not my mum, too. She's all I've got left.*

A Very Brave Girl

The hospital waiting room was lined with hard green plastic chairs, and the only magazines were battered ones with titles like *Crochet World* and *You and Your Cat*. I picked one up, and turned through the pages without really seeing them.

'This is so awful!' Aunt Leona chewed on a nail. 'Oh my God – poor Celia, I hope she's OK – she looked dreadful, didn't she?'

'Mmm,' I said, looking down.

I felt like I might be ill, even though I hadn't eaten

anything in hours. It was all so sickeningly familiar – the nurses rushing about, the antiseptic smell, the fear gnawing at my stomach. Dad had practically lived here when I was nine. I swallowed hard, staring down at an article about whether de-clawing cats was inhumane.

'They've been an awfully long time with her, haven't they?' Aunt Leona twisted around in her seat, frowning. 'What do you think they're doing?'

I turned a page and didn't answer.

After a while, Aunt Leona took the hint and went off to the hospital shop, where she bought a proper magazine and some chocolate. She read the mag in silence, flipping through the glossy pages. She didn't offer to share the chocolate with me.

Every hour or so, a nurse would pop along and thank us for being patient, and tell us they were still doing tests. Finally, when we had been there for over five hours and it was almost nine o'clock, a grey-haired nurse came and got us. 'If you'll follow me, I'll take you in to see the doctor.'

'Is she OK?' cried Aunt Leona, jumping up.

'The doctor will explain everything.'

I put my magazine down and stood up. I felt light-headed, as if I were floating down the corridor after the nurse. Aunt Leona's face looked tense. She kept twisting a plait around her finger.

We got to an office and the nurse showed us in. A brown-skinned man wearing a white coat stood up and offered his hand. 'Hello, I'm Dr Sarjeem . . . please sit down.'

I could barely look at him, I was so nervous. I huddled onto one of the chairs. I was still wearing my school uniform, and I smoothed my hands over my skirt. It was all crumpled and creased by then.

Dr Sarjeem's chair squeaked a bit as he sat down and picked up a file. I could see Mum's name on it: *Celia Pollock.* I couldn't stop staring at it. It was like they had known she was coming.

'You're Sadie?' he asked, opening the file and smiling at me.

I licked my lips, and nodded.

'Right, Sadie. Well, I know how scared you must have been to see your mum collapse like that, but you were a very brave girl. You did the right thing to call the ambulance.'

'I was the one who found her, actually . . .' Aunt Leona reddened as Dr Sarjeem looked at her. 'Sorry, I was just—'

'Will she be OK?' I blurted out.

The top of Dr Sarjeem's head shone smooth and brown. He nodded. 'Yes, we think so. But I'm afraid she's very ill.'

My throat was like the beach, full of choking pebbles. 'What— what's—?'

'We've done some tests on her – an EMG, and a few others – and she has something called Guillain-Barré Syndrome. Or GBS for short.'

Aunt Leona and I stared at each other. 'What does that mean?' I whispered.

Dr Sarjeem leaned forward, resting his elbows on

his knees. 'GBS is an acute autoimmune disease of the peripheral nerves – now, what that means in plain English is that the nerves in her arms and legs have become inflamed. We don't really know why this condition occurs, but the end result is that she's temporarily lost the use of her legs, and her arms will probably follow suit. She mentioned that she's been dropping things a lot recently—'

'Yes, loads of glasses and things . . .' I trailed off, feeling punched in the stomach. *It's just carelessness, that's all.*

'What do you mean? She's paralysed?' Aunt Leona's voice sounded too loud for the small office.

Dr Sarjeem nodded. 'Yes, that's right. GBS tends to go away on its own, but it can take some time, and of course good medical care helps.'

'But – but it goes away? She'll be OK?' My whole body held its breath.

He smiled at me. 'It's likely that she'll make a full recovery. It will just take time.'

Oh, thank God. Oh, thank you, God. I slumped back in my seat.

'So . . . how long?' asked Aunt Leona, biting a nail.

Dr Sarjeem turned to her. 'I'm afraid we can't say exactly. It can go away in weeks, or in months. For most patients, though, around three months seems average.'

Three months?

'Can she come home?' I asked.

Dr Sarjeem's moustache moved as he gave me a sad smile. 'No, I'm afraid not. Sometimes patients have a hard time breathing with the disease, so we need to keep her in hospital until she's well. But of course you can visit her. It's very helpful if you do, in fact.'

Aunt Leona's mouth dropped open. 'But – but she has a business! She can't just be in hospital for months at a time!'

He frowned and picked up a pen with a slim brown hand, tapping it on his desk. 'Well, these are details that will need to be worked out. It's very important that Mrs Pollock's mind is at ease while she's here. She shouldn't be worried about anything; this can affect how quickly she recovers.'

I looked quickly at Aunt Leona. The relief I had felt just seconds ago faded. How could things be so normal yesterday, and so completely wrong now?

Aunt Leona opened and closed her mouth. 'But – but hang on, are you saying *I* should run her business? But I'm meant to be going on – I mean—' She stopped, wings of red sweeping up her thin face.

Dr Sarjeem stood up with a polite smile. 'I do not know your situation, so I cannot say. But I do find that it is at times like this when family can be so helpful.'

Isn't That Wonderful of Her?

A different nurse led us briskly through a maze of corridors to see Mum. Our reflections wavered at our feet as we followed her. I walked tightly, holding onto myself. Aunt Leona's high-heeled sandals clicked against the floor like she was tap dancing, her face screwed up in a worried frown.

When we got to Mum's room, she lay tucked up in a hospital bed, looking as pale as the sheets. I hugged her hard, and tried not to notice the weakness of her arms when she hugged me back.

'Mum, are you OK?'

She gave a sort of laugh and tried to tuck my hair behind my ear. I swallowed and squeezed her fingers.

'Yes, I'm fine,' she said. 'Well, not *fine*, but it doesn't hurt at all. They say it doesn't, sometimes, with this . . . GBS, or whatever it is.'

'I've never even *heard* of it,' said Aunt Leona. She scraped a plastic chair over to Mum's bedside, and gave Mum a lopsided smile. 'Trust you to be so original.'

'Well, it wasn't on purpose,' said Mum wryly. She patted the bed beside her, and I sat down, still holding her hand. It was such a relief to see her looking halfway normal, like she was just having a bit of a lie-down. Maybe this wouldn't be so bad. OK, she'd be stuck here in bed for three months, but I'd come and see her every day. Everything would be fine.

'Have you eaten?' she asked me.

I had forgotten that food even existed. I shook my head. 'No. I'm not hungry.'

'We'll pick up something on the way home,' said Aunt Leona. She fiddled with a bit of hair, rubbing her head. 'Celia, um . . . not to worry you or anything, but what's going to happen with Grace's? The doctor said you could be in here for three months.'

Mum hesitated, glancing at me. 'Sadie, would you give us a few minutes while we talk?'

I stood up slowly. 'Where am I supposed to go?'

Aunt Leona dug into her jeans pocket and handed me a pound coin. 'Here, go and get me a coffee or something.'

Ooh, I'd love to. I took the pound and left the room. But then once I got out in the hallway, I couldn't help myself. I leaned against the wall like I was waiting for someone, and listened to the voices drifting out from the open doorway.

'So what's going to happen, then?' said Aunt Leona.

There was a sound like Mum shifting in bed. 'Well . . . I was hoping that maybe you could stay at Grace's over the summer and take care of things for me. So that I won't have to close down the B&B until I'm well, and Sadie has someone to stay with her.'

I could practically hear Aunt Leona squirming. 'Um, well . . . I want to help, Celia, *of course* I do, but – I mean, I have university, and – well, it's all sort of difficult right now.' She laughed nervously. 'Isn't there anyone else?'

The selfish cow! It was all I could do not to rush back into the room and start shouting at her.

Mum sounded taken aback. 'No, not really – not with Frank gone. It's not like we have loads of relatives. Are you going back to university, then? You haven't mentioned it—'

31

'Well, I was sort of planning to. And – well, it's *completely* petty, and not really an issue at all, but then there's the holiday with Ron—'

'But you said you weren't going!'

'Well, I know, but I thought I might. But like I said, that's totally, completely beside the point – university would really be the sticking point—'

'Well, I don't really know what we're going to do otherwise.'

Silence. My pulse beat against my neck.

Mum's voice lowered. I strained to hear, my nails gouging against my palms. 'Leona, listen – I know you have your own life, but . . . but I just barely manage to pay the mortgage as it is every month. I can't afford to close down while I'm ill; I'd have to refund money to dozens of people, and I just don't have it—'

My stomach dipped. I had known we weren't rich, of course . . . but God. Were things really that bad?

Aunt Leona's voice sounded like every word was being pulled out of her with a fishhook. 'Oh, Celia, I'm sorry . . . I – well, of course I'll help. I'd be glad to.'

She didn't *sound* glad.

I heard Mum exhale. 'Thank you.'

'But I don't know anything at all about it. Blimey, you're likely to go under altogether with me running things.' She forced a laugh. 'I don't even know why you do it; it's not like you enjoy it that much—'

'I *do* it because it was Frank's,' said Mum. 'It's the house he grew up in.'

I nodded in the hallway, my fists clenched.

'Oh, Celia, it's just a house. You're always moaning about how much it costs to run; you'd probably be better off selling it anyway—'

I saw a nurse heading towards me with a questioning look on her face, and I straightened up from the wall and walked quickly away. I found a coffee machine and bought the coffee for Aunt Leona (I didn't spit in it, but I wanted to), and took it back to Mum's room.

'Sadie, Leona's agreed to take care of Grace's while I'm in here,' said Mum, struggling to sit up. 'Isn't that wonderful of her?'

'Great,' I said. I tried not to throw up when I saw Aunt Leona's humble, selfless smile.

'Oh, well . . . anything to help,' she said.

Barf.

Times Change

When Aunt Leona and I got home, it was after eleven and the downstairs was completely quiet. Neither of us said anything as I shut the front door behind us, remembering to lock it up for the night. Dad had painted the door a shiny black, and the locks shone like gold against the dark wood.

Aunt Leona sighed. 'Right, well . . . is there

anything we should be doing, for tomorrow?'

My head was swimming as if I had just staggered off a fairground ride. I touched my forehead, trying to think. 'Just the dining room, I guess. Mum will have done up the guest rooms already.'

She looked relieved. 'Oh, OK. Well, in that case, I'm going to go sort myself out.' And she disappeared like a shot into our flat, her long hair streaming behind her.

I stood alone in the front hallway, and felt like I had missed a step. Um, excuse me, what about the dining room?

I pushed open the door to our flat. Aunt Leona had switched the TV on, and was busy grabbing up her bags and clothes and stuff, which were strewn all over the sofa and floor. She'd been sleeping on our sofa-bed.

'What are you doing?' I asked, staring at her.

She kicked a high-heeled shoe aside, and looked at me in surprise. 'Moving into Celia's room. There's no point my being cramped in here for the next three months, is there?'

As she dragged armfuls of her clothes into Mum's room, I glanced over at the coffee table where Mum had been slumped just a few hours earlier. I gripped my elbows. 'Look, what about the dining room? Are you going to help, or what?'

She reappeared in Mum's doorway, twisting her long hair up in a bun. Her eyes widened. 'But I thought that was your job.'

'It's after eleven o'clock!'

'Oh.' She looked longingly at the TV. 'Well, all right.'

We went into the dining room. The bay window seemed to jump out at us when I switched on the light – a looming black square that swallowed everything. I quickly went over and shut the curtains.

Aunt Leona was standing in the middle of the room as if she had never seen it before. 'Um . . . what do we do first?'

I slid open the heavy top drawer of the sideboard, and handed her a fresh pile of serviettes. 'Here, you can start putting these out.'

Pulling open the second drawer, I gathered up handfuls of silverware, clunking them into the wicker basket. When I turned round, Aunt Leona was folding each serviette into a hasty triangle, laying them down beside the placemats.

'That's not—' I stopped.

Aunt Leona looked up. 'What?'

'Sorry. It's just that that's not how we usually do it.' I started setting out the forks and knives, one on each side of a mat, with a spoon cresting the top.

A line appeared between her eyebrows. 'What do you mean?'

'Nothing; we just usually do it differently.'

'How many ways can there be to fold a napkin, for God's sake?'

I put the basket down on Table One with a clatter. 'Look.' Taking a serviette from her, I started to show her the swan shape. 'You fold it here, and then again here, and then you turn it over, and—'

She let out a short breath, like a laugh that didn't quite make it. 'You're joking! I'm not doing all that, it'll take ages.'

'Fine, OK.' I turned away, and went back to the silverware. And maybe it was stupid, but my hands were shaking slightly as I laid down the forks and knives. Aunt Leona kept moving about the tables, leaving untidy cloth triangles beside each mat. Her mouth was a tight line.

I wasn't going to do anything at first. It's not as though I cared *that* much about the dining room. I mean, I had only ever folded the stupid swans because Mum made me.

But I felt like I was being smothered. I couldn't let the breakfast tables look like that, not with Mum lying in hospital. I put the basket down again.

'What are you doing?' said Aunt Leona suddenly.

'Nothing.' I stared down at the emerging swan, not looking at her.

'You're refolding the serviettes!'

'Look, it's just – I know it's silly, but—'

'I don't believe this! You're actually following along behind me and refolding all the serviettes I've done!' Her face reddened, and her long hair looked wild about her face.

'This is how Dad liked it, that's all.'

She slapped down the rest of her serviettes. 'Well, times change, don't they?'

Tell me about it. I glared at her. 'Look, why don't you finish doing the forks and knives and stuff, and I'll do this?'

Aunt Leona snorted. 'What, so you can come along behind me and redo all of that, too? Forget it! You can do it yourself, if you're so particular.' She strode out of the room, banging the door shut behind her. The oval mirror that hung beside the sideboard shivered.

It was almost midnight before I finished the tables.

The Full English

The next morning I woke up slowly, with a vague feeling of wrongness nagging at me like a sore tooth. My eyes flickered open, and I peered around my room, frowning. It all looked the same as usual – the bright yellow walls that Dad and I had painted, the posters of tennis stars on the walls. My tennis racket stood propped in the corner, gathering dust. I hardly ever played any more, now that Kate was gone.

Suddenly there was a crash from the kitchen, as if a whole pile of pots and pans had hit the floor. 'Bloody hell!' cried Aunt Leona.

What was wrong came smashing back down on me. I jumped out of bed, snatching up my blue-striped dressing gown. I could smell something burning as I ran down the corridor, and when I got to the kitchen I stopped short.

Our old black saucepan lay upside-down on the

floor. Aunt Leona squatted beside it, mopping at a mess of half-fried eggs with a tea towel. Except the tea towel just sort of smeared everything, sliming yolks and egg whites across the tiles like abstract art.

'Oh! This stupid – *stupid* thing—' Aunt Leona stood up and threw the dripping tea towel at the sink. It hit the side of the counter and slid down, leaving a trail of yellow goo.

'I think you might, um . . . need a sponge for that . . .' I trailed off. On the grill, a row of sausages spat viciously, their skins tight and black.

Aunt Leona whirled round at me. 'Don't say a word! Don't say a bloody word!'

'I just meant—'

'Shut up!'

She grabbed up a sponge and started scrubbing the floor, working away at the tiles like she was trying to erase them. Taking a deep breath, I went over to the grill and picked up a fork. But before I could start turning the sausages, Aunt Leona jumped up and shoved me aside, her face red.

'What are you doing? You don't think I can *cook* either?'

'No! These are burning, that's all.'

'They are not.' She grabbed the fork from me and jabbed at the sausages, rolling them sideways. 'They're just a bit crispy on top. They'll be fine.'

I looked at the yellowing piece of paper my dad had taped over the hob. *Fried bread, toast, 1 sausage, 2 eggs, 2 bacon, grilled tomato, mushrooms, hash browns, baked beans.* I could see eggs, bread, bacon and sausage out on the counter, but there was no sign of the rest of the food.

'Um – how many tables are downstairs so far? Because if people are having the Full English Breakfast, you sort of need to cook everything at the same time—'

'*Move*, Sadie,' she said through gritted teeth. 'You can finish cleaning up the floor if you're so bloody certain I can't manage on my own.'

I bent down and quickly sponged up the rest of the sticky eggs. 'But are they?'

Aunt Leona ran the saucepan under the sink. Smoke poured out around us, and she fanned the air, wrinkling her nose. 'Are they *what*?'

I swallowed. 'Having the Full English? Because I'm really not trying to get at you; it's just that—'

She slammed the saucepan back on the hob. 'No! No one's having the Full English! They're lucky to get bacon, eggs and toast, for God's sake!'

'But—' I stood up slowly, staring at her. 'What do you mean? You're not cooking everything on Dad's list?'

'Of course not.' She unwrapped the butter and sliced a piece into the saucepan. 'Frank was a bloody obsessive, and Celia's just as bad. There's no way people expect all that food.'

'But Aunt Leona, they've been staying here for days, some of them! They'll expect to get all the mushrooms and beans and stuff, too – it's not hard, you just have to—'

'And how would you know? Can *you* cook?' She

39

cracked an egg against the side of the saucepan. Bits of shell flaked into the melting butter.

Heat flashed through me. 'Well, it's not exactly rocket science, is it?'

'Oh, so now I'm thick!' She spun round from the hob, hair flying. 'Just get out, Sadie. Leave me alone.'

My bare feet felt sticky where I had trodden in a bit of egg. 'Look, you can't just start changing things! This is Mum's *business*; it has to be done a certain way—'

Aunt Leona slammed the spatula down as the eggs bubbled in the pan. 'You know what, Sadie? *You* can do it, since you know so much.'

'No!' I grabbed her arm as she started to stalk out of the kitchen. 'Aunt Leona, come on! I've never cooked the breakfasts on my own before! All I'm saying is—'

She jerked her arm away, her brown eyes bright with tears. 'All *I'm* saying is, I am *not* a cook, and I am *not* a housekeeper, and I am *not* a bloody people person, and if Celia expects me to do all of this instead of going on holiday, then it has to be on my own terms!' Her voice rose higher and higher, breaking on the last words. She looked seriously close to losing it.

'OK,' I said quickly. 'OK. But . . . but can I help, though?'

Aunt Leona sniffled, scowling. 'I suppose so. But if you say a single word about my cooking, you're on your own.'

Poor Diddums

'Miss, is there some mistake?' The middle-aged man at Table Three peered at his plate with a frown. Light steam from the eggs misted his glasses. 'I ordered the Full English.'

'Yes, I'm sorry. We, um . . . had a problem with our grocery supply.' I had said this to every guest I served breakfast to that morning, but it didn't start sounding any better.

Leaving him scowling down at his bacon and eggs, I gathered up the last of the dirty dishes from the tables, stacking them on my arm as I headed back into the kitchen. The corridor felt still and silent as I passed through it, with sunlight streaming in from the landing window.

'I thought maybe I'd stay at home today.' I put the dishes onto the counter.

Aunt Leona stood at the sink, splashing water about as she did the dishes. She glared at the new ones I had just brought in. 'Oh, ta for that.'

'Is that OK? If I stay at home? It's already after nine anyway.' I was too old to cross my fingers for luck, but I felt like it. School had never seemed quite so pointless, with Mum in hospital. I seriously couldn't deal with another day of *the blonde thing*, not today.

Aunt Leona gave me a look. 'Why should you?'

'Well, I could help you make up all the guest rooms, and then I thought we could—'

'Oh, I see. I need supervision for that as well, do I?' The water churned as she dunked the pile of plates into it.

'No! It's just that you've never done it before. I mean, I haven't either, not on my own, but with two of us—'

'No, Sadie, you cannot stay at home.'

I stood up straight. 'But I thought we could go and see Mum!'

'You can go after school, can't you?' She shoved a plate onto the drying rack. A bit of egg was still stuck to it.

'But—'

'No!' *Splash, slam.* 'And if the school calls and says you're not there, I'll tell them you're bunking off, so don't get any ideas.'

Oh, stop acting all adult; you're only seven years older than me. The words almost burst out of me, like water smashing through a dam. I held them back with an effort.

'Well, will you at least write me a note for being late?'

She smirked at me. 'I'd love to.'

Fuming, I went to take a shower, peeling off the jeans and T-shirt I had thrown on to help with breakfast. The warm water pounded over me like wet needles. I stayed in for ages, soaping and re-soaping myself, until it felt like my skin was shrinking. After I towelled off, I had to climb back into my crumpled uniform from the day before, since my other uniforms were still in the wash.

I went to tell Aunt Leona I was leaving, and found her sitting hunched on the sofa, talking into her mobile. 'Yes, I *know* the flight leaves tonight. Will you stop making me feel guilty?'

Silence for a moment. Aunt Leona groaned and rubbed her temple. 'Oh, I don't know, it depends on Celia. I'd *love* to fly out later if I could, but—' She broke off as she saw me. 'Hang on,' she said, and looked at me with her eyebrows raised.

'I need a note,' I reminded her coldly.

She found a piece of paper and scribbled something on it. 'Here.' She handed it to me, and flopped back against the brown cushions. 'Yes, I know! Oh, Ron, it's *awful* here. I'm sick of it already, and it's only been one day . . .'

I banged the front door after me. Yes, poor diddums, it's all just so awful for you, having to cook breakfast and make up a few beds. As opposed to being in hospital with your legs not working. What had happened to *Oh, poor Celia, I just can't bear it*?

Vampira

Mrs Clark, the school secretary, let out a huge sigh when she saw me. 'Late again, Sadie?'

This was really unfair. I'm not late *that* often. It's just that sometimes I get distracted by the beach on my way to school. But before I could say anything in my defence, the office door opened behind her and Miss Bodley, our form head, walked out. I gulped, and suddenly couldn't say a word.

Everyone calls Miss Bodley 'Vampira', but only behind her back, because no one would ever say it to her face. She was only about five feet tall, but she had paper-white skin, and dark, staring eyes that saw right through you. And she never, ever smiled.

'Is there a problem?' Vampira said.

'Sadie's late again,' Mrs Clark told her, squeaking around in her chair.

'I've – I've got a note.'

I started to hand it to Mrs Clark, but Vampira stepped forward. 'Let's see.'

I handed it to her, and she stared at it like it was a secret document. '*Please excuse Sadie for being late. Sincerely, Leona Harris,*' she read aloud. 'Who's Leona Harris?'

'My aunt.'

Mrs Clark tapped something into the computer, and frowned. 'We don't have her down as a contact name for you.'

Vampira gave me a hard look. 'Are you sure that you didn't just get a friend to write this, Sadie?'

My skin turned hot and prickly. 'No! She's my aunt – my mum's in hospital, and she's staying with me!'

'In hospital?' Mrs Clark's expression struggled

44

between *Oh, dear* and *Right, tell me another one.* She glanced at Vampira.

'Yes, in Brixham Hospital! She's been there since last night. She has something called GBS; she'll be in hospital for ages.' Hot tears leaped to my eyes.

Vampira's expression hardly even changed. 'Come into my office and sit down for a minute, Sadie.' She held her door open for me.

My fingers felt numb as I went into her office. It was like venturing into a graveyard at midnight. *God,* how terrible, to start crying in front of *Vampira,* of all people!

'Your mum's really in hospital, then?'

My head snapped up. 'Yes! You can ring them if you don't believe me!'

She leaned back in her seat. 'That's all right, I believe you. It's nothing serious, I hope?'

'I don't know; she can't move her legs. They say it'll go away, but it might take months . . .' I wiped at my eyes, struggling not to start crying for real. 'Um . . . could I go now? I have to get to class.'

Vampira stared intently at me, as if she were trying to see all the way into my soul. She wasn't all that old – younger than Mum, probably – but her eyes looked as though they'd been narrowed into slits for centuries. Finally she nodded. 'Yes, go on.'

Mrs Clark gave me a late pass after I came out of Vampira's office, and I rushed off, practically running down the corridor. I slowed down once I got away from Reception. I didn't actually have any desire to get to class, especially since I hadn't done any homework.

It was weird – even though I had the perfect excuse for not doing my homework, I didn't want to use it. Telling Vampira had been bad enough. I wasn't about to tell all of my teachers, too, and then have everyone looking at me all sympathetic and worried, asking questions about what GBS was when I didn't have a clue myself. It was scary, that was all I knew. It had paralysed my mum.

The bell was about to ring when I got to my English class. I leaned against the wall and stared over at a display of Year Eight artwork, trying to calm down. I wished that I could just go to the hospital right now, and make sure that Mum was OK.

The bell rang, making me jump. A few seconds later the door opened, and everyone started streaming out in a blur of blue uniforms.

The moment I saw Tara and Hannah, laughing together over some private joke, I knew I couldn't tell them about Mum. They'd be sure to blab it to everyone else, Jan and Alice and all that lot, and I couldn't bear it.

'Did you just get here?' asked Tara. She and Hannah paused when they saw me, and I started walking with them, the three of us jostling our way to PE.

'Yeah, I had to, um – get my eyes tested,' I told them. 'Did I miss anything good?'

Tara laughed. 'Ooh, yeah, if commas are good.'

'Don't confuse her; she hasn't got to those yet,'

said Hannah with a grin. 'So are you going to get glasses, Sadie?'

'You'd look dead *scholarly* with glasses,' said Tara.

'Scholarly Sadie . . . no, I don't think so, actually,' said Hannah.

I put on my 'blonde' face. 'Scholarly Sadie, that's me. Ooh, d'you think wearing specs would raise my IQ up to seventy?'

'Don't count on it,' said Hannah. And we all laughed.

Crawling Ants

When I pushed open the door to Mum's room that afternoon, she lay propped up on pillows, staring at the TV set on the wall. Her brown hair stuck out a bit on the sides, like it does first thing in the morning. An old woman lay in the next bed. I hadn't seen her the night before; a curtain had been drawn around her.

'Sadie!' Mum's face brightened.

I ran over and hugged her, wanting so much to believe that it had all been a horrible nightmare, and that she wasn't that ill, really. And maybe I would even have convinced myself of it, except that she couldn't hug me back. Her hand was like a feeble old lady's as she tried to pat my arm.

'Mum, are you OK?' I sank down onto the bed beside her. The old lady in the next bed peered over at me, and then looked back at the TV screen.

She gave a barking laugh. 'Well, I would say I'm fine, but . . . well, to be honest, my arms seem to be going now, too.'

'Your arms?' I stared down at them.

'I can move them a bit, but not much,' she said grimly. 'God, what a mess.' Her neck twisted as she peered at the doorway. 'Where's Leona? Didn't she come?'

'No, I came straight from school. She'll probably come later.' I tried to fight down the panic that was rising in me. She was worse, and it had only been a day! What did that mean?

'How did breakfast go this morning?'

Dr Sarjeem flashed into my mind, and I stretched a smile across my face. 'Oh, it was OK, actually. Aunt Leona really seemed to be getting the hang of it . . . after a while.'

Surprise and pleasure fought on Mum's face. 'Really?'

'Yeah, she was fine. I mean, I helped her with some of it, but she was really trying.'

Mum's eyebrows lifted, and she nodded thoughtfully. 'Well, that's a relief. Maybe it'll be all right after all, then. Now, tell me how *your* day went. How was your homework; did you do OK?'

My spirits sank like a dropped anchor. Couldn't she ever, ever think of anything else? Then I felt guilty for thinking that, with Mum lying there so weak and helpless.

'Yeah, I did fine. I, um – got eight out of ten for maths.'

I don't know where that came from. I just . . . said it.

All at once Mum's eyes shone like a light had been switched on behind them. 'Sadie! Well done.' Even the woman in the next bed looked pleased.

'Thanks.' My face grew warm as I looked at the plastic water pitcher on her bedside table.

Mum was still smiling. 'See, I knew you had it in you! Now you just need to keep up the good work.'

It felt like ants were crawling all over me. But it was for a good cause, right? Mum's spirits had to be kept up. Dr Sarjeem had said so.

The Dancing Duvet Cover

There was a note on our front door when I got home, stuck to it with a big wad of Blu-tak. I tugged it off, along with the Blu-tak, wiping at the greasy stain with my finger.

Dear Mrs Pollock,

My mum wants me to do a project for school, and I want to do one on business studies, and I thought maybe I could observe your B&B business for the next two weeks and analyse all the areas where you're going wrong—

God! I crumpled it up and shoved it in my bag.

When I got inside, a man with a white moustache was standing in our front hallway, leaning against the wall. He straightened up when he saw me.

'Sorry to hang about; my room's being made up.' He glanced at his watch, his mouth dour. 'Still.'

A feeling of foreboding swept me. It was after four o'clock. Aunt Leona couldn't *still* be doing the guest rooms, could she?

'Oh, right . . .' I edged away from him, smiling. 'I'll just go and see if I can help.'

I dropped my bag and ran up the stairs, rounding the corner. When I got to the first floor, the landing opened out into a pentagon shape – an open space with five white doors, and a stained-glass window showing a sailboat set high up in the wall.

I found Aunt Leona in Room Three. It wasn't difficult; I just followed the sound of swearing.

'OH! This . . . bloody . . . bloody thing . . .'

The door was partly open. I pushed it open the rest of the way and peeked in. Room Three was painted in different shades of green, to go with the view of the garden. And now the pale green duvet cover was standing up on the bed, doing some sort of weird aerobic dance.

'Aunt Leona?'

The duvet cover wriggled about a bit, and Aunt Leona's head popped out. Her cheeks were apple-red.

'*What?*'

I shut the door behind me. 'Um . . . do you need any help?'

50

'No. I am doing perfectly fine, thank you.' Her feet pressed into the mattress as she wrestled with the duvet cover. The duvet slithered heavily out and puddled about her feet.

'Here, should I – maybe if I just hold the duvet for you—'

'Sadie.' Her eyes were glittering and dangerous. 'Get out of this room before I scream.'

I got out. And I stood in the hallway staring at the other four doors on the landing, wondering what they looked like inside. Had she even done them yet? Glancing at the closed door to Room Three (where I could still hear Aunt Leona huffing and puffing about), I walked softly across the pale blue carpet. The doorknob to Room Two turned in my hand, and I slipped inside.

At first glance, the room seemed OK, and my shoulders relaxed. But the more I looked at it, the more I saw that things weren't OK at all.

The fern-patterned duvet cover looked lumpy, and was hanging at a weird angle off the bed. The white wicker waste basket was full of papers and tissues. The coffee and tea caddy on the chest of drawers still had dirty cups on it, and empty, crumpled packets of sugar. I peeked in the en-suite bathroom. A used towel lay on the floor, and there were hairs in the bathtub.

I wasn't some big expert on housework, and normally whether the rooms were made up right was the last thing on the planet I cared about. Because normally Mum was here to do them, nagging me to help and ruining my weekends and holidays.

But now . . . I bit my lip. What if the guests started complaining about how terrible the service had suddenly become, and Mum somehow heard about it? My hands tensed as I saw her lying motionless in her white hospital bed, and before I knew it, I was picking up the towels and grabbing the dirty coffee cups.

'What are you doing?'

I jumped, holding the towels to my chest. Aunt Leona stood in the doorway, glaring at me.

'Nothing – I just thought—'

'You're doing it again, aren't you?' She gritted the words out, her face drained of colour. 'You're following along behind me, redoing what I've done. I don't *believe* this!'

'I'm not! I mean, yes, I am, but – Aunt Leona, you didn't even clean the bathroom.'

Her face flushed. 'I hadn't got to it yet, that's all! Don't you dare try to turn this back on me!'

'Look, you're supposed to totally finish every room, not do them in bits and pieces.' I tried to keep my voice reasonable, but it was difficult. Aunt Leona scowled.

'I'll do them however I feel like it! God, I don't even want to *be* here! I can't believe you're nagging me about the housework now, on top of everything else—'

I threw the towels on the floor. 'It's not just housework!' I shouted. 'Don't you get it? It's Mum's business, and you're ruining it!'

Aunt Leona's face grew redder and redder, like a ripening tomato. 'I am not ruining it!' she yelled. 'I'm trying my best—'

'You're not! You're not cooking the breakfasts right, and people are having to wait for their rooms, and then the rooms look awful – you're not doing *any* of it right!'

Her voice dropped deadly low, trembling. 'That's it, Sadie. I'm not going to stay here and put up with this abuse when I'm trying my best. *You* can just do it all. It's yours.'

She wheeled away from the doorway. A second later I heard her running down the stairs.

Well, fine. At least with her gone, I could get on with it and finish up the rooms. I jerked at the duvet cover, pulling it taut, and rinsed out the coffee cups in the sink. I was just getting clean towels from the linen cupboard on the landing when the man with the white moustache came upstairs, his brown leather shoes whispering against the carpet.

'Excuse me, is my room made up yet? I'm checking out at five a.m. tomorrow, and I need to pack. The lady who just left said I should ask you.'

'Ask me?' I repeated stupidly, clutching the towels.

His moustache came down over his mouth. 'Well, she said she was in too much of a hurry – that she had a flight to catch.'

I stared at him, my arms suddenly cold with goosebumps. 'What . . . ?'

The man let out a breath and shook his head. Moving past me, he peered into Room Two. 'Well, good. About time.' He took the towels from me, and the door closed after him with a *click*.

It had hardly shut before I was racing down the stairs.

Our Dream Day

I ran through our flat, calling Aunt Leona's name and pounding all the doors open. My voice echoed back to me. In Mum's room, the bed was unmade and a dirty teacup sat on the bedside table.

Aunt Leona's suitcases were gone. I rushed to the window and shoved the curtains aside, looking out at the car park. Her red Vauxhall had gone, too.

No! I grabbed for the phone on Mum's bedside table, and dialled her mobile number. A smooth electronic voice cut into the first ring. *I am sorry, but the Goldphone user you are dialling is currently unavailable . . .*

The rest of the afternoon passed in a daze. I paced about the empty flat, biting my nails and trying over and over again to ring Aunt Leona. I left four messages for her, which probably all sounded exactly the same – *I'm really, really sorry, please come back!* I almost started laughing as I was leaving the last one, or crying, or a mix of both. This was just completely mad.

When it started to get dark, I warmed up some frozen chicken nuggets from the freezer, and ate them in front of the TV. A stupid programme about people buying a hotel in France was on. 'We just love it here!' cooed the woman. 'We're so happy; this is our dream day.'

The chicken nuggets tasted like cardboard, catching at my throat. Occasionally I heard the front door open, and I'd jerk up and turn the sound down – but it was always just guests coming in, their soft footsteps heading up the stairs.

After the third time this happened, I sat back tensely on the sofa, chewing my thumbnail as the room pressed around me. Aunt Leona could *not* have actually flown off to the Canaries!

Could she?

Her holiday was for three weeks, she had said so. And meanwhile, I'd . . . I'd what? What would happen if people found out she had left me here? My heart jumped off a cliff, thinking about it.

No, stop it. I grabbed the remote and turned up the volume for the TV. 'Ooh, and just look, we can see the vineyards from our balcony,' the woman gushed. She swept her arm at the view.

I settled down to watch, and tried to ignore the icicles piercing my stomach. There was no way that Aunt Leona would take off on holiday and leave me here. She'd be back by the time I got up in the morning, just like nothing had happened.

You're Hired

Only she wasn't.

The Goldphone user you are dialling . . .

I hung up the phone slowly, the electronic voice

55

echoing in my ear as I stood in the empty lounge. She had really left. No, hang on, be sensible – she *couldn't* have actually gone to the Canaries, so she must just be in London. Maybe just for the day, just to scare me. She'd be back. She would.

I spun round, shaking, as I heard voices come down the stairs and head into the dining room. It was seven o'clock. People were out there wanting breakfast.

And I had to cook it for them. There was no one else.

Forget Aunt Leona, just do it! I rushed into my room to get changed, pulling on jeans and a top. On second thoughts, I swapped the jeans for a pair of black trousers. I scanned myself quickly in the mirror. Thank God I was so tall. Did I look sixteen, though? I grabbed a hair clip and pulled my long blonde hair back in a ponytail, hoping to add a few more years.

As I went back into the kitchen, I could hear more people coming downstairs. Don't panic, just get to work! I pulled the fridge open. Sausages, eggs, tomatoes—

I stopped, staring. Where was the bacon? I hunted through the fridge, shoving juice and milk aside. We *couldn't* have run out of bacon; we never ran out. Or at least we never ran out when Mum was here to do the shopping.

Never mind, I'd skip the bacon. I grabbed the ingredients we did have, and piled them on the counter. Except – except what would happen if someone complained that the breakfasts had gone downhill, and wanted to speak to an adult?

I found Mum's diary, and dialled a number.

'Hello?'

'Marcus, do you still want to help out with our B&B for your report?'

His voice turned squeaky with excitement. 'Yes! You know I do!'

'Well, you're hired. Get over here as soon as you can – and bring bacon.'

'What? Um . . . Sadie, where am I supposed to get bacon?'

'I don't care! Just get as much as you can, and *hurry*.' I hung up. My hands felt numb as I took the notepad from the counter and went into the dining room.

Four of the tables were full, with a couple sitting at each. They looked like all the other gazillions of guests I had seen coming and going over the years. Except that this time *I* had to deal with them.

Looking down at my notepad, I licked my lips and said, 'Hi – um, what would you like for breakfast?'

The couple at Table Four looked tanned and healthy, like sailors or golfers. 'Two Full English Breakfasts,' said the man, unfolding his serviette. He wore a gold signet ring on his pinky. 'And we'd like the *Full* English this morning, please.'

'Have you any Earl Grey tea?' asked his wife. She had sleek brown hair, and wore little pearl earrings.

'Um . . . I think so.' I wrote it down.

She snapped her menu shut and handed it to me. Her mouth looked pinched. 'Also, we don't like to complain, but our room wasn't made up yesterday.'

Heat throbbed at my temples. I had forgotten about finishing up the rooms yesterday after Aunt Leona had left. God, how could I be so stupid?

'Oh, I'm – I'm sorry,' I stammered. 'It's just that my mum is ill . . .'

At the next table, a woman with silvery hair leaned over. 'Actually, our room wasn't made up either,' she said apologetically.

'They'll all get done today, I promise,' I said, clenching the notepad.

Pushing the rooms out of my head for now, I took the rest of the orders. A few minutes later I headed back into the kitchen, my head spinning with *Full English, no hash browns* and *scrambled eggs, not fried.*

Marcus stood at the back door, peering in through the window. I ran for it, pulling it open. He was clutching two packs of bacon to his chest. 'I've got some!' His glasses sat askew on his nose. 'My mum had a couple of packs—'

'Oh, thank God!' I grabbed them from him and plunged into cooking, feverishly melting butter and breaking eggs into the frying pan.

Marcus straightened his glasses with a finger. 'What should I do?'

'Um, you could start making some toast. No, wait—' I grabbed him as he headed for the bread. 'Pour some orange juice into the jugs first, they're in that cabinet – and start making the tea and coffee.'

He tutted. 'Sadie, this doesn't seem very well

organized. Don't you have a plan or something that you follow?'

'No, I don't. Just do it!'

He pulled a small notebook out of his back pocket and wrote something in it. I grabbed it off him and chucked it onto the counter. 'Marcus, come on! Juice, coffee!'

His mouth pursed. 'All *right*. You don't have to shout.'

When we got the first few breakfasts done, I took them to the dining room with my heart jammed in my throat. Please God, let my cooking be OK, even though I'd had to pick bits of shell out of the eggs and the first batch of mushrooms got burned.

'I ordered scrambled eggs,' said the man at Table Five, frowning down at the plate I had put in front of him.

'Oh, I'm sorry, I— I forgot to tell my mum,' I gasped. 'I'll take it back and ask her to redo it—' I reached for the plate.

He made a face. 'No, don't bother.'

'I'm really sorry,' I muttered. I wrote it down, and I still managed to get it wrong! My face burned as I hurried back towards the kitchen. I almost ran into two women who had just come downstairs.

'Oh, sorry! If you'll just sit down, I'll be there in a minute—'

The older one gave me a stiff smile. 'Fine. And do you suppose our room might get made up today? We're out of fresh towels.'

But That's Illegal

It was like that until almost nine-thirty, with Marcus and me racing about the kitchen, and me taking plate after plate out – and then suddenly I realized that everyone had eaten, and the place was starting to empty. That's what always happened. People didn't hang about at the B&B, they wanted to get out and do things for the day.

'You know, you could actually help with this bit,' I said to Marcus as I carried in a pile of dishes and teetered them beside the sink. He was leaning against the fridge, writing painstakingly in his notebook.

The light sparkled off his spectacles as he looked up. 'You could be bringing in those dishes a lot more efficiently, Sadie.'

'Yes, too right! *You* could be helping me.'

The shrill of the phone pierced the air. Aunt Leona! I started to grab it, and then stopped as my fingers touched the receiver. No, hang on – what if it was school, asking where I was?

Ring-ring! Ring-ring!

Think! What was Aunt Leona's voice like? Not as low as Mum's, plus she had this stupid, drawling London accent now that she'd lived there for two years.

I picked up the phone. 'Hello, Grace's Place.'

'Yes, hello, this is Mrs Clark from Drake Secondary

School. Is that Mrs Harris?'

'*Miss* Harris, actually,' I said snootily in my Aunt Leona voice.

'Oh – sorry. I was just ringing to check on Sadie; she wasn't present when we took the register this morning.'

I twined the cord around my fingers. 'No, she's ill; I was just going to ring.'

'Oh, dear . . . what's wrong with her?' Mrs Clark sounded like she was writing something down.

Marcus stared at me from across the kitchen. I half-turned away. 'I'm not sure; some sort of bug – she was up all night, being sick. She might be out for a few days, actually.'

'I see. Well, will you be picking up her schoolwork for her, so she can keep up?'

'Oh – well, yes, if I have time. I'm very busy at the moment, running this B&B for my sister—'

'Or we could have one of her friends drop the work by.'

No way! If Hannah or that lot got wind of what had happened, the whole school would know in an hour.

'No, that's all right, I'll come by. Or – or you never know, she might be better after today.'

'Well, we'll ring again tomorrow if we don't see her, just to check.'

When I hung up the phone, my palms were wet. I sank against the kitchen counter.

'Sadie, what's going on?' Marcus's eyes were almost the size of his glasses.

61

I bit my lip. 'Um . . . well, I think I'm in really big trouble.'

His eyes bulged. 'What have you done?'

'*I* haven't done anything, you berk! It's my aunt, she's left!' I explained about Mum being in hospital, and what had happened with Aunt Leona, and he gaped at me.

'But that's illegal,' he said. 'She can't just leave you.'

'Well, she has done, funnily enough.'

'Well, you should tell her it's illegal, and that she could go to jail.' He folded his arms over his chest, looking like a midget headmaster.

I opened my mouth to say something, and then closed it as the phone rang again. I picked up the receiver. 'Hello?'

'Sadie?' Aunt Leona's voice sounded scratchy and far away.

I jerked up straight. 'Aunt Leona! Where are you?'

'The— the Canaries.'

A cold chill gripped me. 'You didn't really go there!'

'Sadie, I'm sorry! I'm so sorry, I shouldn't have come; I've made an awful mistake – I was so angry that I wasn't thinking, and then the plane took off and it was too late—'

'Come back! Can't you come back?'

Her voice sounded shrill, panicked. 'I've been trying all morning! But the return flight's already paid for; it costs hundreds of pounds to change it, and I don't have any money! I'm over the limit on all my charge cards—'

'What about Ron?'

'You're joking; he hasn't got any money! I think he took out a loan or something for the holiday.'

'Then use Mum's bank card; can't you do that?' Mum had given Aunt Leona her bank card at the hospital, to do the shopping with.

'I can't! I checked this morning, and she's only got about forty pounds in the account. Besides, if I did that she'd know I went, and – and I don't want her to know. Don't tell her, OK? Sadie, promise me!'

Marcus stood in front of me, mouthing, 'Tell her she could go to jail!'

I turned away, clenching the phone. 'Well, what am I supposed to say to her? I think she'll *notice* that you're not about!'

'I'll ring her. I'll pretend I'm there or something.'

Sand grated my throat. 'So you've flown off to the Canaries on holiday and you're not coming back, is that what you're saying?'

'I *can't*, that's what I'm saying! I'm stuck here for the whole three weeks! Oh, Sadie, I'm sorry; are you going to be OK?'

'No! How could I be? I can't run a B&B on my own! I—'

'Sadie, hang on, you're fading . . . I think my battery's dying . . .'

A river of static flowed down the phone, prickling my ear. And then Aunt Leona was gone.

I hung the phone up slowly, shaking.

'You didn't tell her she could be arrested,' said Marcus sternly.

'Marcus, not now; I have to think!' I paced about the kitchen, biting my thumb. What was I going to do? I couldn't handle this on my own. I had to tell Mum, no matter what Aunt Leona said.

But what would happen if I did? I stopped pacing and looked around me at the shiny white cabinets that my dad had painted, imagining Aunt Leona being arrested. Me taken into care. The B&B closed down for months, not making any money, when we hardly had any to start with.

Mum's frightened voice: *I'd have to give refunds to dozens of people, and I just don't have the money* . . .

I scraped both hands through my hair. 'Marcus, look, I'm – I'm just going to have to run the B&B on my own for a while. Until Aunt Leona's back.'

His face lit up. 'Cool! Can I help?'

'Yes, but you can't tell anyone, OK? It's hugely important. *No one* can know she's not here.'

'I won't tell anybody!' He was practically quivering with excitement. 'This is great; we can do loads of stuff on our own – work out marketing plans, and—'

'I don't *care* about marketing plans, Marcus! We just can't let anyone know what's going on, that's all – and God, what about school? I can't be ill until the holidays; they'll send someone to check. I have to go back so they won't suspect anything, only I *can't* be at school and do this, too—' Panic strangled my voice.

Marcus opened up his notebook and straightened his glasses. 'Right,' he said. 'This is not a problem. We can figure it out. We just need to decide on a plan of action.'

Mum's Handbag

'*Lost* it?' Mum struggled to sit up and failed, falling back against her pillow. 'Is she sure?'

I nodded, unable to meet her eyes. 'Yeah, she says she left your bank card at the shops yesterday, but not to worry, 'cause she rang the bank and cancelled it last night. But she wondered if you had any cash to buy groceries with for a couple of days.'

'Well, my handbag should be in that closet.' Mum shook her head, frowning. 'Has she ordered a new card, then?'

'I guess.' The bit about leaving it at the shops had been Marcus's idea – his mum had done the same thing a few months ago.

I found Mum's handbag and brought it over to the bed. I felt so awful lying to her, but I didn't know what else to do. I had to buy groceries for tomorrow. And I only had about six pounds.

Mum shifted. 'Have a look in my wallet.'

I snapped open her red leather wallet with the

Scotty dog on it. 'You've got . . . thirty pounds. And some change.'

'Right, well, give her that – it won't last long, though. Tell her to let me know if the new bank card doesn't arrive soon.' Her dark eyebrows were knitted worriedly together.

'OK.' I put the money in my pocket, looking down. 'Um, she said she'd ring you soon. She's just sort of busy with Grace's, that's all.'

Mum let out a breath. 'She's annoyed because she has to run it for me, isn't she? That's why she hasn't been to see me again.'

I licked my lips. 'Well—'

'Oh, you don't have to tell me; I know what she's like. I wish I could go shake some sense into her, but of course if I could do that I wouldn't be in here, would I? I can't even ring her myself now, my arms have got so bad.'

I swallowed, glancing down at her arms. 'Can't . . . can't you move them?'

'No.' Mum glared at the ceiling. 'God, I'm going mad already, and it's only been a few days! Never mind . . . how are *you* doing? How was your day?' Her brown eyes bored into me.

I managed a smile. 'Oh – it was great.' And it actually hadn't been bad, apart from worrying about how I was going to manage on my own for three weeks without anyone finding out about it. I'd rather clean rooms with Marcus than go to school, any day.

I didn't tell her that bit. Instead, when she asked

how I had done on my homework, I told her that I had done really well. Ten out of ten on my maths *and* Mrs Green had read my English essay out loud to the class.

It sounded so good. I wished it were all true, and not just a lie to cheer Mum up.

'Sadie!' Mum beamed. 'You'll have to bring it in and read it to me.'

My stomach lurched. Oh God, of course she'd want to *see* some of this fabulous work. What had I done? 'Well – she's displaying it on the board at school now, but yeah, I'll bring it in soon.'

She was still smiling when I left.

Fun with Learning

Thirty-eight pounds sounds like a lot, but it doesn't buy a whole bunch of groceries, as I found out when I went to the store on my way home. I shopped for ages, frantically doing sums in my head (which were probably all wrong anyway) and getting the cheapest of everything I could. But I was still only able to buy enough breakfast stuff for the next few days, and that came to £36.38. I almost broke my arms dragging it all home, too.

I was just putting everything away in the kitchen when the doorbell rang. I froze, my hand on one of the cupboard handles. What if it was someone wanting to check in? I was still wearing my school uniform! I ran to my room and threw on my black trousers, yanking a red T-shirt over my white school shirt.

The doorbell rang again, and I went out to the door, holding my head up and trying to look at least eighteen.

Marcus's mum stood there, wearing baggy trousers and a faded blue shirt. 'Hello, Sadie,' said Mrs Marcus. (I didn't actually know Marcus's surname; it was something so boring that I forgot it every time I heard it.)

'Is your aunt in?'

'No, she's at the shops,' I said quickly.

Mrs Marcus looked exactly like her son – very thin, with big glasses and lank brown hair. 'Well, I just wanted to thank her for letting Marcus research his project here. He's so excited to be analysing a business close up!'

'Oh, that's OK.'

'It really is extremely kind of her, when she must have so much else on her mind – with your mum in hospital.'

I couldn't think what to say to that. If I agreed that Aunt Leona was extremely kind, I might throw up. I managed a smile.

'Do you think she'll be home soon?'

My fingers tightened on the doorframe. 'No, she was going to stop by the hospital and see Mum.'

Mrs Marcus looked concerned. 'Oh, of course.

Well, maybe I'll catch her tomorrow . . . are you *sure* she doesn't mind if Marcus is here all day again? He says she doesn't, but it seems such an imposition that I just wanted to check.'

My nails gouged into the black-painted wood. 'No, not at all! She said he's so . . . so bright and outgoing, and such a big help – she loved having him here! He can come for as long as he wants, she said!' Talk about over the top. I could have stapled my tongue to my lips.

But Mrs Marcus beamed. 'Oh, that's very kind of her! Yes, Marcus is a special boy, isn't he?'

That's the word for it. I nodded.

'Oh—' She pulled something out of a plastic carrier bag tucked under her arm. 'I got him this, by the way. You can show your aunt.' She handed me a bright blue book. *How to Run a Perfect B&B,* by Greg R. Smeed. 'I thought it would be fun for him to compare the theory with the practice.'

'That . . . sounds great,' I said, staring down at the book.

She backed away a step. 'Tell your aunt I'll see her soon. And if I can do anything to help out, with your mum so poorly, just tell her to let me know.'

'I will.' I watched Mrs Marcus head down the path towards her own house, the orange streetlights glinting off her spectacles.

I bet life is just so educational at Marcus's house.

Canary Yellow

Just as I was about to close the door, a grey car pulled up in our drive. I ducked back quickly, shutting the door, and pressed against it with my heart crashing about in my chest. Those really *were* guests!

Right, stay calm. Remember the plan of action. When the doorbell rang again I took a shaky breath and opened the door, wiping my clammy hand on my trousers.

A young dark-haired couple stood on the doorstep smiling at me. 'Hi, we're Mr and Mrs Hoffman,' said the woman. 'We've got a room reserved.'

'Come in.' I held the door open, and they trundled into the hallway, rolling a matching set of blue leather luggage after them.

'Can you check us in, or do we need to see your mum?' asked Mr Hoffman.

I kept a pleasant smile on my face. 'No, I can do it. I help her out a lot.'

Before they could argue, I went into our flat and got Mum's red reservations book. I flipped the pages open to the week of July 3rd, and found their name scrawled across the boxes for Wednesday and Thursday in Mum's loopy handwriting. I took the book back out into the hallway. 'Right, um – so you're staying for two nights, right?'

Mr Hoffman nodded, glancing behind me at the door to our flat. 'Are you sure we don't need to see your mother?'

'She's not here, she's in hospital.' My voice came out sharper than I had meant.

The Hoffmans looked taken aback. 'I hope it's nothing serious—' started Mrs Hoffman.

I gripped the book. 'No, I mean – my aunt's here, helping out, but she's gone to the shops. I help out all the time, though. I've checked people in loads of times.'

Mr Hoffman nodded quickly. 'Yes, sorry. I mean, that's fine.' He looked as though he seriously wished he had never brought the subject up.

I stared down at their reservation, trying to look like I knew what I was doing. What did Mum do next? I cleared my throat. 'The room's thirty pounds a night . . .' And then I saw that Mum had written *chq recv'd* under their name. Cheque received, maybe? '. . . but – but you've already paid?'

'Yes, that's right,' said Mrs Hoffman.

'So, um . . .' I looked down at the book again, but it didn't give me any clues as to what came next. I could feel them both staring at me, and heat crept up my neck and arms. Then, like a lifeline, I saw the sheaf of canary-yellow check-in forms stuck into a flap at the back of the reservations book.

I tugged one out with a smile of relief, and handed it to them. 'You just need to fill one of these in – there's a pen on the table over there. And then I can escort you up to your room.' That was what Mum always said, only it sounded a lot better coming from her. I saw Mrs Hoffman hide a smile.

Never mind. I ducked back into our flat, and grabbed the key to Room Six from the row of hooks hanging above Mum's desk. A few minutes later we were climbing the stairs.

'Oh, how lovely!' exclaimed Mrs Hoffman as we rounded the curve and she saw the stained-glass window of the sailboat. Its colours in the sun shone like half-sucked lollies.

Suddenly I saw Dad standing up on a ladder, grinning down at me and saying, 'Pretty good, eh? Just like being in church.'

A lump lodged in my throat. 'Thanks,' I said, looking away. 'Um – your room is on the second floor.'

Splurge on the Jam

'"Breakfast at a B&B establishment is, for many guests, the focal point of their visit, the thing that they will remember as positive or negative through-out their entire stay."' Marcus stood in front of the fridge, reading aloud with one finger trailing along the page.

I swore as a splash of grease from the frying pan leaped out. The yolk had broken on one of the eggs, slithering out in a yellow ribbon. The baked beans bubbled away in a saucepan next to them, splattering the hob.

'"Therefore, it is of utmost importance that a good impression is made. Splurge on the expensive jam, the silver toast rack. The very best farm-made sausages should not be too good for your guests."'

'Marcus, stop reading that thing at me!'

He squinted at the grill, where a row of sausages sizzled. 'What kind are those?'

I shoved him away with my elbow as I prodded at the sausages with a knife, jumping back as they spat grease at me. 'Oh, the very best farm-made, *of course*. Haven't you done the toast yet?'

He put bread in the toaster with one hand, still reading out loud. 'And, listen to this: "Ensure that the food on the plates is laid out in a pleasing manner. Remember that your guests will first devour their food with their eyes, and you want their first impression to be a favourable one." Sadie, you haven't even *thought* about this; yesterday you were just slapping everything on the plates!'

I was about to slap *him* on the head. I waved my hand in the smoky air, and turned the grill down. 'You need to slice the mushrooms for me, Marcus. Which means you need to put that stupid book down and *get on with it.*'

His glasses were two circles of mist. He tutted, not even looking up. 'My mum said that if I'm to get the most out of this experience, I need to compare the theory with the practice, and—'

God! I grabbed up a knife myself, chopping mushrooms. 'Well, in practice, everything else is ready, and it's going to all be *cold* if I don't get the mushrooms fried!'

Finally it was all done. A quick last check of Dad's list, and then I scooped up the first two plates and took them into the dining room, plastering a smile on my face. *I'm just so happy to be here. I love helping out my aunt at our happy B&B.*

Mr Morrison, the man in Room Five, stifled a yawn as I put his plate in front of him. 'Why did your aunt decide to change the latest time for breakfast? Eight-fifteen's quite a jump from nine o'clock.'

I wiped my hands on my apron. It was one of Mum's, with blue and white stripes on it. 'Oh – because my mum's in hospital, and my aunt's just helping out. She has to get to work in the mornings.'

Mrs Morrison made an *oh, that's too bad* face, cradling a cup of coffee in her hands. 'What's wrong with your mum?'

I hesitated, and refilled her husband's coffee from the pot on the sideboard. Five of the other tables were full, and half of the guests were yawning and clutching their coffee cups like lifelines. They had all got our note, obviously – printed out by Marcus on our ancient computer and slipped under their doors yesterday.

'Oh, she'll be fine . . . she just has to stay in hospital for a while.'

'What's wrong with her, though?'

I stiffened, and glanced over my shoulder towards the kitchen. 'Oh, sorry – I think I hear my aunt calling.'

Any Time, My Dear

When I got to school that morning, Hannah and the others were hanging about outside the doors in a laughing blue cluster.

'Sadie!' Hannah waved me over. 'Did you see that makeover show last night?'

Alice's eyes gleamed. 'We were just talking about that first woman's outfit – *what* a mistake! Did you see it?'

'Oh – um, just the last bit.'

'Did you see the bit where they gave her a makeover, and she burst into tears?' asked Tara, tucking a bit of red hair behind her ear.

I made my eyes go big, shaking my head. 'Blimey, how bad was she to start with if she cried *after* the makeover?' Everyone laughed. I hadn't actually seen the show; I had been too busy having fun with our industrial iron, pressing all the clean sheets I had washed.

When there was a break in the conversation, I turned to Hannah, touching her arm. 'Listen, um – I sort of didn't get a chance to do my history worksheet last night. Do you think—' My face caught fire. Hannah didn't even seem bothered.

'Sure, here.' She pulled it out of her bag and handed it to me. While the others kept talking, I sat on a bench to one side and hurriedly copied the answers, my pen wobbling a bit on the wooden slats. Don't think about what you're doing, just do it! Think how happy it'll make Mum to see a good paper for once . . .

The bell pierced through the air just as I scrawled the last answer. I handed the sheet back to Hannah. 'Thanks.'

'Any time, my dear,' she drawled.

Scientific Hoovering

'Sadie, how are you feeling?' Mrs Clark beckoned me over to her desk as I walked inside.

She wouldn't mention Mum, would she? I glanced back at the others, and let out a breath when I saw they hadn't waited for me. But I felt a bit empty, too. Tara would wait for Hannah, or Alice for Jan.

'Oh, I'm OK. It was just a twenty-four-hour thing, my aunt said.'

'Yes, there's some of those going around at the moment . . . and have you heard any more news about your mum?' Her eyes widened.

'No, nothing,' I said tonelessly.

She nodded, her plump face just a little disappointed. 'I see. Well, you'd better hurry and get to your first lesson.'

When the bell rang for lunch, I avoided Hannah and Tara and ran out to the courtyard. I made my way to the back gate, weaving through groups of kids laughing, talking, playing football. I had found out the day before that Marcus couldn't make a bed to save his life, so our plan of action called for him to do as much of the cleaning as he could on his own in the mornings, and then for me to come home at lunch and do the rest of it.

Nobody in the courtyard paid me a blind bit of notice. I let myself out onto the footpath and started to run.

A few minutes later I burst through the back door of Grace's. 'Marcus?'

No answer. I found him sat in front of our ageing computer in the corner of the lounge, typing away with his feet swinging off the edge of the chair.

'Marcus, what about our plan of action? You're supposed to have all the hoovering and everything done by now!'

He turned round, squinting at me. 'I've already done it. I'm just setting up a website for Grace's.'

'What? What for?' I grabbed up a pile of fresh towels.

'Because it's important.' Marcus scooped up the book and flipped through it. '"It is vital that you stay current with certain trends. Some customers depend solely upon the Internet to book their holidays, and you don't want to miss out on their business through being a technophobe! A website can—"'

I took the book away and pulled him up by his arm. 'I'm going to shred that thing if you don't stop reading it at me! Now come on, help me!'

He ran after me as I pummelled up the stairs. 'Did anyone see you?' I asked as we made up the double bed in Room Two. Or as I did, really.

His thin face turned smug. 'No. I did it exactly like we planned. I kept really careful watch, and then when each room left for the day I snuck into it and started hoovering with the door shut. It's actually very scientific, you know. Hoovering.'

'Great.' *Snap, snap* – I pulled the sheet and duvet firm, fluffing the pillows up. Room Two was decorated in a soft blue, to go with a big watercolour of the sea that Dad had picked up at a local auction. Mum hated it, but she hadn't touched it since he died.

I rushed into the bathroom to give everything a quick wipe and a tidy. Marcus was still talking.

'I bet no one's ever done a proper study on it. But you can increase your efficiency *loads*, probably as much as twenty per cent, if you're careful to do it all at right angles, and—'

God, it was enough to know he hadn't been seen; I didn't need to hear all the scientific details! Using the master key, I let myself into the next room and started again. Thankfully only four rooms had people staying over that night; I could leave the rest the way they were for now.

The moment I snapped the last duvet into place, I scooped up the dirty towels and ran down the stairs. Throw them in the washing-machine, chuck some soap in, punch it on—

'Can I stay and work on my website?' asked Marcus, adjusting his glasses. 'I've got a great idea for it. See, I'm going to—'

'Yes, that's great!' I grabbed an apple from our fruit bowl and took off at a run, banging the door shut behind me.

The P Word

My lungs on fire, I pounded up the hill and turned into the school drive, my bag whacking against my legs with every step. The building looked like a ghost town.

The second bell rang just as I got to the front steps. No! I jogged around the side of the building and slipped in the door next to the canteen. It creaked shut behind me.

I just had to get to science. And Mr Jenkins was on his own personal planet half the time, so I might, just might, be able to slip in without him noticing. I walked quickly through the corridors, keeping my head down.

Which was how I almost walked straight into Vampira.

'Oh!' I started, stopping up short.

She stared at me with her dark, emotionless eyes. 'Why aren't you in class, Sadie?'

'I'm sorry, miss. I was in the loo.' Oh, please God, don't let me still smell of bathroom cleaner, or she'll wonder what I was doing in there.

Vampira frowned. 'Are you sure? You're five minutes late to class, and you look very flushed. Have you been running?'

'No, I was in the loo! I was— I was crying.'

Her frown faded slightly, and I hurtled on. 'I didn't want anyone to know, but I'm just really worried about my mum – she can't move her arms either now, and . . .'

I gulped. I thought I really might start crying then.

Vampira nodded. 'I understand. Would you like to sit in my office for a bit, until you feel better?'

'No! I mean, no, please, miss – I should just get to class.'

Her mouth moved. I don't know if it was meant to be a smile or not. Probably not. 'All right, then, Sadie. Go on, but don't let this happen again.'

I was so shaky after that that I really did go to the loo, just to take a few deep breaths and calm down. I was splashing water on my face when the door opened and Milly walked in, her dark hair pulled back in a rough ponytail.

Surprise fell across her face. 'Oh. Hi.'

'Hi,' I muttered, thinking, *Oh, great, Miss Perfect Marks. Just what I need.* I rubbed my face on the rough cloth of the towel dispenser, not looking at her.

'What are you doing, hiding out?' She leaned against one of the sinks.

My gaze snapped to hers in the mirror. 'What do you mean?'

She grinned, and pointed at the floor. 'Well, you've got your bag with you. So it looks like you haven't been to class yet this afternoon, right?'

I made a face. 'Excellent deduction, Sherlock.'

'Yeah, you know what he always said – once you eliminate the impossible, you're left with the truth, however unlikely. Or something like that. Sorry, that's a paraphrase.'

Did she have to show off even in the girl's loo? 'I really wouldn't know.'

She sat on one hip, swinging her leg. 'Well, not everyone's into old Arthur C. D., but he's a pretty good read. I mean, if you're into that sort of thing.'

Oh, go lick off the Battleship's whiteboards. I pressed my mouth together with the effort not to say it. 'What are *you* doing in here, anyway? I mean, since you're obviously not going to the loo.'

Her thick eyebrows rose. 'I'm hiding out too, can't you tell? Mr Jenkins looked like he was about to get me to read my poem out to everyone.'

'What poem?'

'Oh, just a poem I wrote, about atoms. He heard Mrs Green going on about it. Anyway, here's a tip –

if you ever want to get out of a class, just say that you think you've started your period; they'll let you out in about two seconds flat. Some days I start my period three or four times. You have to keep track, though, or else they start thinking you have medical problems.'

Heat swept up my face. I had only had my period for about six months, and it really wasn't my favourite topic of conversation.

Milly waggled her eyebrows. 'Especially the male teachers, they practically pass out if you mention the P word.'

Looking away, I picked up my bag. 'Right, well, I'm late enough as it is.'

She smiled wickedly. 'What are you going to say? That you've got the P word?'

'No, I'm going to say I was crying in the girl's loo.'

Milly tilted her head to one side and nodded, pursing her lips together. 'Crying . . . yeah, I guess that could work, too.'

100 Years of Caring

When I got to the hospital that afternoon, Mum's bed was empty.

I stood in the doorway staring at it dumbly, wondering if I had the right room. But no, there was her roommate, Greta, the old lady who had had the stroke. Greta looked up at me, and I backed away in confusion, banging the door shut. My heart felt like it might hammer through my chest. Where was Mum? What had they done with her?

A nurse stood a few feet away checking something on a trolley, her back to me. I ran over to her. 'Excuse me – I'm looking for my mum – I don't know where my mum is—'

She turned round, and glanced at Mum's closed door. 'Mrs Pollock, is it?'

I nodded, my throat dry.

'Wait here; I'll find out where she is for you.' She strode briskly off to a sort of podium halfway down the corridor, where two other nurses stood talking. A minute later she was back.

'Your mum's in surgery, and then we'll be moving her to Intensive Care. You really should have been notified, but I suppose there wasn't any time – she's been finding it hard to breathe, you see, so they're inserting a tube in her throat to help her out a bit.'

The blood fell from my face. I couldn't say anything.

The nurse touched my arm. She had blue eyes, and a nametag that read *Brenda Jones, RN.* 'It's not as scary as it sounds. This sometimes happens with GBS; I'm sure the doctor will have explained it to you.'

'When— when can I see her?'

Brenda looked as if she wanted to hug me. I was glad she didn't, or I would have started bawling.

'Well, she'll be out of surgery soon, but she'll be

very groggy after that. Why don't you leave a note for her at the nurse's station, and we'll read it to her once she's awake? Then you can see her tomorrow.' She touched my arm again and walked away.

In a daze, I found the nurse's station and borrowed some paper and a pen. *Brixham Hospital, over 100 years of caring for Brixham,* the paper said on it. I stood staring at it for ages, until the words blurred wetly together and didn't make any sense at all.

'Are you all right?' asked the nurse behind the desk.

I nodded. Clearing my throat, I wrote carefully, clutching the pen.

Dear Mum,

   I'm sorry you've had surgery and hope you feel better soon. Don't worry about anything, everything is OK at Grace's and Aunt Leona is doing a really good job running things.

   Love,

   Sadie xx

   PS – I got an almost perfect score on my history homework today.

That's Only Five Per Cent

Marcus was still in the lounge when I got home, tapping away at the computer. It was a relief to have him there, actually. Being alone just then . . . I swallowed.

He twisted round in our creaky old computer chair to look at me. 'Your mum doesn't have Dreamweaver, does she?'

'Have what?' My voice sounded scratchy, like I had a raging cold.

'It's a software package. I can build the site in Express, but it's not as good. And I want to do a really flash site, so that people can book their own reservations and stuff.'

'Oh.'

He stared at me. 'Sadie . . . Dreamweaver?'

'Um, I don't know.'

Marcus sighed and went back to his typing. 'A couple of people rang to make reservations today.'

My hands iced. 'You didn't answer the phone, did you?'

'Of course not! I let the machine pick it up, just like we planned.'

Glancing at the machine, I saw that the little green light was flashing. The plan was for me to ring people back using my grown-up voice, but instead I just stared at the light, watching it go on and off. I felt like I had been disconnected from my body.

'What's wrong? You're acting all weird.' Marcus was watching me.

'I'm just—' I let out a breath. 'Just – worried about Mum, that's all.'

'Oh.' He blinked. 'Well . . . what's that thing that she's got called again, and we'll look it up on Google.'

I went over to stand behind him, looking over his shoulder. 'GBS.'

'What does that stand for?' He was already typing it onto the screen.

'I don't know! Just GBS.'

It was enough. The very first hit that came up said, *GBS – Guillain-Barré Syndrome Support Group.*

'Here, let me sit down.' I slid into the chair, staring at the screen.

But then I hardly knew where to start. The site had pages and pages of information, all of it in small, pressed-together writing. There were long words everywhere I looked. My stomach pitched sideways. I was never going to be able to understand all of this.

'Try that one.' Marcus pointed at a button that said, *GBS Explained.*

So I clicked on it, and suddenly my eyes were stumbling over words like *toxin exposure, cerebrospinal, electromyogram.* They felt like scorpions crawling over me. And then I saw it: *Death in GBS is a rare event, occurring in about 1 in 20 cases.*

The world froze. My heart froze.

'Oh, hey, that's not too bad,' said Marcus, reading over my shoulder. 'One in twenty, that's only five per cent. Statistically, you've got nothing to worry about.'

Shut up! Shut up! But I couldn't say it. I couldn't say anything.

Complications

Marcus had to leave after that, to get home in time for his tea. I didn't eat anything. I would have vomited it straight back up again, all over the keyboard, because *one in twenty* didn't exactly sound rare to me. *Rare* would be *one in two million,* not one in twenty. I blinked back tears, hating the site, hating whoever had written it.

Death tends to occur more commonly in elderly people severely affected by GBS, but like any other illness, unexpected complications can arise. Death is more likely to be a result of a complication rather than GBS itself.

What did that mean? What was a 'complication', exactly? I sat biting a hangnail, staring at the screen. Did it mean that once you had GBS, other things could really affect you, and you might die? Dr Sarjeem flashed into my mind. *She shouldn't be worried about anything while she's in here.*

If Mum found out that Aunt Leona had left me alone for three weeks, what would it do to her?

All of a sudden, my dad's funeral came rushing back: the strangling smell of flowers, and the round-faced vicar who droned on and on about the tragedy of God calling one of his flock home so young. Afterwards, it had seemed like everyone cried except Mum, who stood still and silent, staring at the coffin. I'd started crying then too, partly because Dad was gone, but also just because I was so scared of the look on Mum's face.

And now in my mind I was back at the funeral, only this time it was Mum lying in the coffin.

Ice choked my heart. What would happen if Mum died? If she found out what her own sister had done, would that make her so much worse that she might become the one in twenty?

My fingers clutched the hard plastic mouse. I'd be an orphan, completely alone. I'd be sent away to live with strangers, or in a home somewhere. They'd have to sell our house. Dad's house. *Mum would be gone.*

The screen blurred. For a second I seriously wanted to ring the police. I wanted to tell them what Aunt Leona had done, so they'd track her down in the Canaries and arrest her, and then her face would be splashed across every paper in the country as she was dragged off to prison.

But I couldn't do that. Mum was depending on me, whether she knew it or not.

Wiping my eyes, I clicked another page on the website and kept reading.

Cycling in the Pyrenees

'Excuse me.' I reached across one of the two women at Table Three to get her plate. They were the same two women I had almost run down in the corridor the other day. They were all smiles now, nodding politely to me as they went on with their conversation.

'Yes, such amazing views,' said the older one. 'So still and quiet, as if the rest of the world doesn't even exist.'

A headache smashed my temples as I glanced at my watch. Eight forty-three, and they were still sitting there yakking away! I really didn't need this, not after staying up until almost two o'clock that morning, reading about all the horrible things that could happen to Mum.

The younger one smiled at me, obviously wondering why I was hanging about. *Because it's late, everyone else has left, and you're still drinking your coffee!*

'We're just talking about our last cycling trip, up in the Pyrenees,' she said. 'Completely stunning mountains. We both love Spain . . . brilliant skiing up there, as well.'

Fab. 'Um, I'm sorry to hurry you, but my aunt—'

'We're here to do the South West Coast Path now,' put in the older one. 'Just for a bit of a holiday, after the Pyrenees!' They both laughed, *chortle chortle*. Oh, leave!

Finally they drifted back up to their room, still nattering away about cycling. I whipped their dishes off the table and ran into the kitchen with them.

I had exactly six minutes to get changed and get to school.

A Very Famous Triptych

The window in the artroom door was dark, which meant Mr Grange was presenting one of his history of art slide shows again. I softly eased open the door, hoping I could just slip in and sit in the back. Of course Mr Grange spotted me the second he saw the light from the hallway angling in. He's young and blond; half the girls in our group fancy him.

'Sadie, you're late – is there a problem?' He peered at me through the beam of light from the projector.

My face went red instantly, but at least the room was so dark you could hardly tell. I went over to the table where he had the slide machine set up. 'Sorry, sir,' I whispered. 'It's just that I, um – started my period.'

I could not *believe* I'd said that. But it worked – suddenly Mr Grange looked like he had swallowed a hot pepper, even in the dim light. 'Oh, I see. You don't need to – see the nurse, or—'

I shook my head vehemently, praying that no one else was hearing any of this.

'Well, that's fine, then,' he said. 'Just take a seat, Sadie.'

The light shifted as the slides clicked forward. 'Right! And here we have *The Adoration of the Lamb*, a very famous triptych by the Van Eyck brothers . . .' He sounded very relieved to be talking about art again.

Milly caught my eye as I started towards the back of the room, and smiled. My face flamed and I looked away, sinking down next to Hannah and Tara.

Tara squinted at me in the gloom. 'Where were you?' she whispered.

I kept my eyes on my bag as I settled it onto floor. 'Mrs Clark wanted to talk to me.'

'What for?'

'I don't know. Some form that Mum's supposed to fill out.'

'Quiet, girls,' called Mr Grange. 'Now, still in the Flanders school, there's the work of . . .'

I folded my arms on the desk, leaning towards Hannah across the table. 'Um, Hannah . . . I sort of didn't get my maths done last night . . .'

I had hardly even finished the sentence before Hannah was pulling a paper out of her folder. I copied it quickly, keeping an eye on Mr Grange.

Exactly the Same

'Now, it's not as bad as it looks, all right?' Brenda turned to look at me, her blue nurse's uniform rustling slightly.

I swallowed. 'Yes, OK.'

'But I'm glad I caught you before you went in, because you should be prepared. The thing is, the tracheostomy – that's the operation we did to put the tube in your mum's throat, to help her breathe – makes it impossible for her to speak.'

'I— I know,' I managed to get out. The GBS website had gone on and on about it.

Brenda squeezed my shoulder. 'Sadie, I know how scary that sounds, but it's only temporary; I promise.'

We had stopped walking by then, standing in front of Mum's closed door. A nurse carrying a clipboard hurried past.

'There's a GBS volunteer in with her now,' said Brenda. 'Someone who's had this condition herself, and knows what it's like first hand. She'll help you work out a way to communicate with your mum until she's better; there are codes and things you can work out.'

Somehow I managed not to turn on my heel and run for the lift. Brenda put her arm around me. 'She'll be OK, love, really. Now come on, are you ready to see her?'

She gave me a little squeeze, and I nodded, even though going into that room was the very last thing I wanted to do. 'Good girl. Now, I have to go check on another patient, but call me if you need me, right?'

Brenda bustled off, leaving me there alone. I took a deep breath and reached for the doorknob.

Mum lay on her bed as still as a plank of wood. She didn't even turn her head when I went in. And I had thought that the tube would be like a slender snake, but it was *massive* – a clunky white accordion-tube of plastic had taken over her throat, plugging her into a black and silver machine beside her bed. Another smaller tube led from her nose to a drip on a stand.

I started as a woman at Mum's bedside stood up, and came over to me with her hand out. I hadn't even noticed her.

'Are you Sadie?'

I nodded. I couldn't have said anything to save my life. Or Mum's life, come to that.

She was tall, with short grey hair and warm, lively brown eyes. 'Sadie, I'm Tricia. I had GBS myself a few years ago.'

'Will she be OK?' I blurted out. I couldn't stop looking at Mum, lying there like a giant, motionless doll. Her chest moved gently up and down. Was that the machine breathing for her?

'Let's step outside for a moment,' murmured Tricia. She turned to Mum, and said, 'We'll be right back, Celia,' in this completely natural voice, as if we were all out on a jolly shopping spree together.

We sat in the waiting area, and Tricia leaned towards me, her voice intense. 'Now Sadie, listen to me. I know how frightening this must look, but the thing you have to remember is that *it's still your mum in there*. She can't move; that's all. But she's aware of everything that's going on around her; she's still *thinking*. She's still exactly the same person.'

A hot lump lodged in my throat, and I wiped my eyes with my hand. Tricia patted at the pockets of her sundress. 'Oh, I'm sorry, I don't have a tissue—'

'That's OK,' I mumbled. 'Will she be all right, though? I saw – saw this website, and it said that one in twenty people die from this . . .'

Tricia squeezed my hand. 'That's statistically true, but I don't think it will happen in your mum's case.'

'You don't know, though!' I jerked my hand away as my voice rose. Across the room, an old man reading a magazine looked up.

'No, that's true,' said Tricia calmly. 'Nobody can *know*, Sadie.'

Neither of us said anything. For a few minutes, the only sounds were the old man turning pages, and nurses passing by.

Finally, Tricia touched my arm. 'Come on, let's sit with your mum, and I'll show you how she can communicate with you.'

Blinking Hard

Tricia stayed with me as I sat with Mum. I'm not sure I could have done it otherwise. Mum just – just *lay* there, still and quiet, her eyes following my every word. I babbled away, on and on, terrified of the utter silence that would drop around us if I stopped talking.

'And look, I wanted to show you this – see, I got a nine out of ten.' I fumbled in my bag, and held up a maths paper I had copied from Hannah. The

Battleship had written *Good work!* at the top.

'Oh, lovely!' said Tricia from the other side of the bed. 'She's done well, Celia, hasn't she?'

Mum's lips moved in a smile. *Yes*, she blinked.

That's how she communicated: blinking. Once for yes, twice for no. You could do the alphabet too, apparently, but that took a while.

I looked down and shoved the paper away, crumpling it in my bag. Tricia kept smiling at me, and my chest felt like an anvil was sitting on it. 'Yeah, Mrs Shipton says I've really improved.'

Yes, blinked Mum again. Which I guessed meant *fantastic, well done, I'm so proud of you.* I hoped so, anyway. I kept talking for almost half an hour, telling her everything I could think of that would make her happy.

I even managed to laugh once or twice.

Angel Wishes

That night I stood staring into the fridge, leaning my temple against the cool plastic door. No matter how long I stood there, it didn't look any better. Three packs of bacon. Two packs of sausages, two measly cartons of eggs . . . barely enough for breakfast over the weekend, and then that was it.

And I didn't have any more money.

'Should I get more bacon from Mum?' Marcus was

hovering at my elbow, looking worried.

'No, she'll start wondering what's going on. We'll just have to – to figure it out, somehow.'

Marcus glanced at the scanty contents of the fridge. He started to say something, and then thought better of it.

The fridge door made a sucking noise as I shut it. Think, Sadie, think! I needed money, and fast. The thing was, most people made a reservation before they came, and sent a cheque for a deposit. And then once they got here, they usually wanted to write a cheque for the rest of it.

We had got seven cheques by then, totalling over two hundred pounds, which *sounded* fantastic. But even though I could deposit them into Mum's bank account, no problem – I had dropped by Brixham Building Society after school on Thursday – I couldn't get hold of the money afterwards, because Mum's bank card was lying on a beach in the Canaries. It was like sending money into a black hole.

I let out a breath, and scraped my hair back with both hands. 'Maybe – maybe I could get some of the guests to pay cash when they check in.'

Marcus twisted up his face. 'Maybe . . . but people don't like paying cash very much. If they don't pay by cheque, then they like using their credit cards, because then they can get air miles and special offers and things like that.'

'Hang on . . .' I muttered, staring at him. 'Marcus, that's it!'

'What? What?' He ran after me as I bolted into my bedroom.

When I was eleven or so, I went through this stage where I thought I might be artistic, and I still had some poster board and markers left over. I dug them out of my wardrobe, and found a sheet of white A4 cardboard.

'*Sa*-die . . . what are you doing?'

In neat red letters, I wrote, *Ask about our special offer!* I handed the sign to Marcus. 'Put that in the front window, OK?'

'What special offer?' His nose wrinkled as he squinted at the sign.

'The one that's going to buy breakfast for us, with any luck.'

Marcus looked doubtful, but he went and put the sign up. The white square looked very small against the window. Staring at it, I crossed my fingers and kissed them. Dad used to call it an 'angel wish'.

Not that I believed in angels, but I'd take any help that was going.

Rate of Fall

The weekend was a complete holiday after all that I had been doing – two whole days when I didn't have to try to get back to school on time after lunch. Doing up the rooms was simple when I didn't have to race about like an Olympic runner.

It didn't last long, though. It was Monday again before I knew it, and then I was running again. Even once I got to school, I still had to run – Miss Fitch, our PE teacher, had everyone outside doing timed sprints in the sizzling heat that afternoon. She was obsessed with 'healthy competition'.

I had run a really good time when she last timed us doing the sprints, back around Easter, so I was one of the first to go. With the sun streaming down on me, I pounded down the field as fast as I could, and Miss Fitch clicked her stopwatch.

'Sadie, you've improved your best time by four seconds; well done! Have you been practising?'

'Oh – not really, miss.' Just panicking on a regular basis.

As the others did their sprints, I sat cross-legged on the warm grass a little way away, and carefully pulled Hannah's science homework out of my bag. Taking out a pen, I started to copy out her answers into my book.

Explain three ways that outside forces can affect an object's rate of fall. *Weight can affect an object's rate of fall, because when something is heavier, it—*

A shadow fell over my exercise book. Snapping it quickly shut, I looked up.

'Hi.' Milly sat down beside me on the grass. 'I thought you were into this sort of thing.' She pointed over to where some people were running extra sprints for fun – Chris DeBacca and that lot.

'Yeah, I just had some homework to do.' I shoved my exercise book deep into my bag, hoping that Hannah's name wasn't showing.

'Well, don't let me stop you.' She swiped at a strand of hair that had come loose from her clasp.

'That's OK; I'll do it later.'

She redid her ponytail, scraping her thick hair back with both hands. She glanced over at me as she refastened it. 'Why do you keep copying Hannah's homework?'

I struggled to sound normal. 'I don't. What do you mean?'

'Oh, come on, Sadie. I've seen you do it loads of times.' She leaned back on the grass, crossing her ankles.

'What, are you watching my every *move* now?' I forced out a laugh. 'Anyway, you're mad; I don't copy from Hannah.'

Milly's eyes were very clear and grey in the July sunshine. 'Sadie. I don't *care* if you copy, OK? I'm not going to turn you in or anything. I just wondered why you do it, when you're miles cleverer than Hannah is.'

I gaped at her. 'You're insane! I'm not cleverer than Hannah.'

'Sure you are. Have you ever talked to Hannah? She's about as interesting as a damp sponge.'

'Of course I've talked to her! Have *you* seen my marks?'

She shrugged. 'Marks aren't everything.'

'Well, you could fool me.'

Milly sat quietly on the grass, watching me. 'Anyway, I bet you could do a lot better if you wanted to. Maybe you're just not trying hard enough.'

Oh, God, not *that* again. 'You know, if I had a pound for every time someone's told me that, I could fly to Tahiti and lounge on the beach for the rest of my life! I mean seriously, I could even afford someone to follow me about and carry my *towel* for me.'

Milly shook her head, half smiling to herself.

'What?' I snapped.

'Sadie, no one with your sense of humour could be thick, OK? It's, like, scientifically impossible.'

Miss Fitch's voice floated to us from across the field. 'Faster! Come on, pick up those feet!'

I swallowed hard. 'Well . . . well, then explain why I'm so crap at school, if you think I'm so clever. Because I *do* try. I try really hard, and I still get pathetic marks.'

Milly squinted her eyes up, nodding slowly. 'Now *that's* interesting.'

'Oh, please continue, Sherlock.'

She sat up and crossed her legs. 'Well, you're definitely not thick. So if you try but still can't get good marks, there must be a reason for it.'

'Like what?'

'I don't know; maybe you have dyslexia. Or maybe you just try too hard.'

I snorted. 'You can't try *too* hard.'

'Sure you can, if you're getting all wound up over

it. Like, I used to take piano, and I was *awful* at it. And I had to play at a recital, and I practised so much that I practically made myself sick, and then when I got out on stage I just froze. Dad said if I had just relaxed and had fun, I would have done a million times better.'

The casual way she said 'Dad' was like a fish-hook in my heart. I looked down, plucking at a blade of grass. 'You can't relax and have fun with schoolwork, though.'

She raised an eyebrow. 'Can't you? Why not, then?'

I opened my mouth to answer and then shut it again, thinking of the hours and hours I had spent struggling at my desk, trying to get the answers right, knowing they were completely wrong. And Mum saying, *Sadie, come on, you're not concentrating.*

Fun. Right. She was from a different planet. Tearing the grass in two, I threw the pieces away and stood up.

'You just can't, that's all,' I said.

Our Sadie

There were only a couple of people left to do sprints by then, with the rest of the class all milling about and watching. I went over to the side of the field and stood with Hannah and Tara. Alice was there, too, watching as Jan ran her sprint. Everyone was laughing, cheering her on.

'What were you talking to Milly about?' asked Tara.

I applauded with the others as Jan huffed her way past Miss Fitch, her round cheeks red. 'Oh, nothing. She just came over and sat with me.'

Alice glanced over at me. 'You looked really serious, the pair of you. You were talking for ages.'

Hannah nudged her. 'Yeah, they have so much in common – Sadie and Milly!'

The three of them started laughing, looking at me with shining eyes like they expected me to join in. *Ooh, yes, I'm just so bwainy!* But it felt like my chest had turned to stone.

'What do you mean?'

Hannah stopped laughing abruptly, looking surprised. 'Well, just that – you know. Milly's such a swot, and you . . .' She trailed off.

'I'm really thick, you mean,' I said.

'No, not *thick* – just—' Hannah's face turned red.

Tara gave me a hug, rumpling my hair. 'You're our Sadie and we love you,' she said. 'We wouldn't have you any other way.'

Special Offer

The woman who rang the doorbell that afternoon peered at me with cold grey eyes, clutching a black leather handbag with both hands.

'Have you got any rooms? We're looking to stay

for a week or two.' She had a scattering of tiny white whiskers on her chin, and permed old-lady blue hair. She looked like she had spent the last seven hours going from B&B to B&B, comparing prices with her nose crinkled up.

My fingers tightened on the door. 'I think we might have one. I mean, I'd have to ask my aunt; she's actually running things, but—'

'And what's your special offer?'

I tried to sound casual, as if we had twelve people a day asking about it. 'Oh, it's just that if you pay cash, you get ten pounds off a night.'

Her black pencilled-in eyebrows flew up. 'Really! So that would be—'

'Twenty pounds a night.'

She peered past me into the hallway, checking out the house. 'Could I see a room?'

'Sure.' I glanced at her car, where I could see a spindly white-haired man sitting behind the steering wheel, reading a paper. Apparently he wasn't being invited in, as well. Maybe he didn't get an opinion.

Looking in the reservations book, I saw that Room Seven was empty, so I took her up to it. There was a massive wardrobe that Dad had sanded down and stained, and yellow flowered wallpaper. I drew back the cream-coloured curtains, and showed her the view of the ocean sparkling in the bay.

I could tell that she was trying not to look impressed. 'Is it available until the twenty-first?'

Oh, God, if you pay cash, you can stay as long as

you like! 'Yes, I think so . . . I'll have to ask.'

Strangely enough, my phantom aunt said that yes, the room was available, and could I possibly be the one to check them in, since she was very busy doing something extremely important? So I gave them a registration card to fill out – Mr and Mrs Dumont, from Newbury – and handed them their key.

'I hope you enjoy your stay.' My smile was real, stretching across my face.

Mrs Dumont took the key from me. 'Yes, thank you,' she said stiffly. 'I hope so, too.'

Intensive Bed-Making Class

'Right.' I ripped the duvet and sheets off my bed. Air currents rippled through the room, ruffling Marcus's hair.

'Time for intensive bed-making class.' I handed him the pile of bedding. 'Look, it's really not hard – see, you just pull everything up as tight as you can . . .'

Marcus gripped the sheet with his fingers and tugged sideways. 'Like this?'

'Sort of . . . no, look, you pull *up*. Just pull it all up really tight. Come on, Marcus – if you get this I won't have to come home at lunch any more.' I tried to laugh.

We worked on it for over an hour, but it was as though his hands just wouldn't do what they were supposed to. He really tried – twitching the covers this way and that, muttering to himself. But when he finished, my bed looked like an entire pre-school had been bouncing up and down on it.

'Um . . . I think that looks OK, don't you?' He glanced at me hopefully.

'No, it doesn't look OK at all!' I ripped the duvet off, feeling hot and sweaty. 'It looks *awful*. God, Marcus, you're meant to be so clever! How come you can't *make a bed*?'

He shifted feet. 'I don't know. It just . . . doesn't seem very logical.'

'But—' I stopped, seeing his face. 'Oh, never mind! I'll just have to keep coming home.'

How, though? No matter how fast I ran, I still got back to school panting and late after cleaning the rooms. I was running out of excuses. I'd used the period story again that afternoon, on Mrs Green in English, and I felt sick every time I thought about it. I was sure to get caught soon, even though there were only eight school days left of term.

Would she and Mr Grange compare notes on something like that? Sitting in the staff room – *Guess what, Sadie Pollock got her period today! Oh, did she really? That's funny, she got it last week, too.*

'Anyway, are we finished now?' Marcus pushed his glasses up with a finger. 'I want to show you something.'

I fluffed the pillow up, punching at the feathers with my fist.

'*Sa*-die . . .'

I sighed, and tossed my pillow onto the bed. 'Yes, all right.'

Mr Brochu

Two minutes later Marcus was sitting in front of the computer, tapping away. 'Right, now watch this.'

How come his hands were so agile on a keyboard, but turned to mush if you put them anywhere near a duvet? And then the screen flickered, and I forgot about making up the rooms.

'Marcus, that's amazing!'

There was a photo of our house on a green background, with *GRACE'S PLACE, BED & BREAKFAST EXTRAORDINAIRE!* written under it.

Marcus grinned at me, his glasses shining in the light. 'Ta-da! Your new website!' He clicked through it, showing me photo after photo of the inside of the house. The stained-glass window. The garden. He even had a photo of Dad on there – the one that sat on our coffee table, where he was holding a paintbrush up and grinning.

I leaned forward, drinking it in. 'This is fantastic! Did you really do it yourself?'

His skinny chest pushed out. 'Sure, it's easy. It actually went live last night; I was just working out a few kinks. And look, they can even make their own reservations on it.' He pointed the cursor at a dark green button that said *Reservations*. A second later a new screen came up, with a calendar page on it.

'Oh, wow!' he squeaked. 'Someone's already made a reservation for Friday week! Look – *Mr and Mrs John Brochu.*'

A feeling like a slow-motion car crash rocked through me. 'Marcus . . . did you check the reservations book first?'

He blinked. 'Um . . .'

I grabbed up the book, flipping through it, and groaned. 'Here, look – we're already completely full that Friday night; we've got a hen party coming to stay!'

'A what?'

'A *hen party*. It's like a party before a wedding – look, you'll just have to tell Mr Brochu that he can't come; we don't have any rooms.'

Marcus bit his lip, looking at the screen. 'Well . . . what about your mum's room?'

My teeth clenched. 'We are not using my mother's room, Marcus. Forget it.'

'But it's just sitting there empty. It might be empty for months and months.'

I put the reservations book back onto the coffee table, trying to hide the fact that my hands were shaking suddenly. 'Well, we're still not going to use it, end of story.'

'That's not very logical of you, Sadie.'

'I don't *have* to be logical!' I snapped.

'But you have a room! A completely vacant room, with no one in it for ages. The professional thing to do would be—'

'Marcus, stop it! Just write to Mr Brochu and tell him, all right?'

Heaving a huge, martyred sigh, Marcus swung the chair back towards the screen and started typing while I read over his shoulder. *Dear Mr Brochu . . . We are very sorry, but . . .*'

'That's good,' I said finally. 'Tell him to ring if he wants to come on a different date.'

Marcus typed the words in, then clicked the mouse to send the email. He frowned, and clicked it again.

'What?' I said.

'Um, I'm not sure . . .' *click, click, click.* 'The email doesn't seem to be responding. It's, like, hung up or something.'

'*Mar*-cus . . .' I said threateningly.

'No, hang on.' Tapping the mouse. 'There, it's gone.'

'Are you sure? Are you positive?'

'Yes, I'm sure! He's not coming now, even though you have an empty room he could stay in.' Marcus switched the computer off and stood up, looking like a cat who'd had a mouse taken away from it. 'And I have to go home now.'

I grabbed his shoulders and shoved him back down. 'No way. Not before you take off that reservations thing.'

His jaw fell open. 'But it took me ages!'

'Marcus, I don't care. If guests can book rooms

when we don't *have* any rooms, it's not exactly a good thing, is it?'

He did it, but he was not filled with joy. He was far too young to know half the words he was muttering to himself.

The Industrial Revolution

That night I sat at my desk staring at my homework. With the end of term looming, some of the teachers were going berserk. There was an RE essay that I couldn't copy off Hannah, and an essay for history that I had to do as well – loads of stuff. I felt nauseous just thinking about it all.

The Industrial Revolution was a watershed time in English history. Discuss three ways in which it affected day-to-day life. For instance, how did it affect the average housewife doing the shopping?

All at once an idea flew into my head, and I sat staring at the book without seeing it. Of course! How totally obvious!

Taking a fresh sheet of paper, I made up a menu, listing everything we offered for breakfast – hash browns, bacon, tomatoes, the lot. I had noticed that some people told you when they didn't want something, like no mushrooms or whatever, but other people didn't, they just left what they didn't want on their plates. And that was a waste of food, wasn't it?

Please tick the items you would like for breakfast, and put this list outside your door before 7 a.m. This will let us prepare the meal to your complete satisfaction.

Perfect, that made it sound like I was doing *them* a favour. But if we knew that someone never wanted mushrooms, and they stayed for a week, then we could save almost a pound. And that was only one person. I bet we could save hundreds of pounds a year, doing this!

My gaze fell on my history book again, and the elation drained out of me. I pushed the paper to one side.

Yeah, great idea. Shame I was so thick when it came to school.

Take Your Cozzies

'Here you go – two Full English Breakfasts.' I smiled at the last two guests as I put their plates in front of them. Mr and Mrs Chambers, from Cardiff. They had checked in the day before, and they looked like twins, with the same dark hair and matching sports shirts.

'We were wondering if we could have a quick word with your aunt?' said Mrs Chambers as she unfolded her swan.

My smile hardly even wavered. Another week had

passed, and I had miraculously managed not to get caught. I was a complete pro at deflecting this question now. 'Oh, I'm afraid you've just missed her – she's gone to the shops.'

Mr Chambers took a sip of orange juice. 'Well, maybe you could help us. We were just wondering what there is to do in the area.'

At first it felt like when one of the teachers called on me in class, but then I said slowly, 'Well – there's the Coast Path; that's really good.'

Their eyes lit up. 'Oh, have you been on it?' said Mrs Chambers.

'Yes, loads of times. It starts practically just outside our door. Once, my dad and I even hiked all the way down to Dartmouth.'

'But isn't it awfully difficult?' asked Mr Chambers.

'No, it's fine if you have the right shoes.'

Suddenly they were throwing loads of questions at me. They even got out a guidebook, so I could show them the places where the path got really steep. (There are bits you practically *fall* down instead of walking down.)

'There's an old quarry on a side-trail about a mile from here, just before Berry Head; we used to go poking around in there sometimes. And then there's a great beach just about here.' I pointed at their book. 'You should take your cozzies if you go. It's freezing, but it feels fantastic when you're all hot and sweaty.' I grinned, remembering Dad floating on his back in the ocean, spraying water up like a whale.

111

'Thanks, Sadie, that's great.' Mr Chambers stood up finally, pushing his empty plate away.

'Yes, that's brilliant – we'll take your advice.' His wife smiled at me as they left the room, and I started gathering their plates up. And then I got back into the kitchen and saw the clock, and my smile faded like melting butter.

It was after nine o'clock.

'No!' I gasped. 'Marcus, why didn't you tell me what time it was?'

'What?' He looked up from the computer, blinking.

Calm. This is not a big deal. All you have to do is ring the school; you've done it before. Filling my lungs with Aunt-Leona air, I picked up the phone and dialled.

'Good morning, Drake Secondary.'

'Yes, hello. This is Leona Harris, Sadie Pollock's aunt—'

'*Oh*, yes, hello. We were just about to ring.' Mrs Clark sounded like she was chewing a lemon.

Icy needles scattered over my arms. 'Yes, um, Sadie's going to be late this morning. She had to – help me out with something, but she'll be in soon.'

I hung up before Mrs Clark could say anything else, and then stared at the phone. I had a very, very bad feeling about this. Why hadn't I just said I was ill, and taken the day off?

Withered Old Crone

I walked the long way to school, going around the building so that I could avoid the front doors completely. The door beside the library was silent, abandoned. I eased it open and hurried through the corridors, my footsteps raining around me. Oh God, please don't let me run into Vampira again.

I was in luck; there was no sign of her. But then when I got to my class, the Battleship stopped talking and stared at me. 'Yes, Sadie?'

'Um – sorry I'm late, miss.'

She looked at me for a long moment, her arms crossed over her chest. I stood tightly in the doorway, waiting for the nuclear warhead to explode.

'Do you have your homework?' she asked.

'Yes, miss.' Hannah had done her maths the day before, when we had a library period, and Tara and I had copied it then.

'Give it here, please.' She held out a wrinkled hand.

I could feel everyone watching me as I fumbled with the zip on my rucksack. Finally I managed to pull the paper out of my folder, and handed it to her. She took it and went over to her desk, leaning over a pile of papers.

What was going on? I glanced over at Hannah and Tara. Both of their faces were on fire, and Tara looked like she was about to cry. Behind me, I could feel Milly trying to catch my eye. I didn't look at her.

The Battleship straightened up. 'Thank you, Sadie,' she said coldly. 'Please sit down now.'

I swallowed and sat down, not looking at anyone. Had she sussed that I was cheating? But why hadn't she said anything if she had? My lungs clenched. Oh God, what if Mum found out I had been cheating?

The lesson droned on like nothing had happened. Except that it was obvious something had. Hannah, Tara and I sat silently at our table, not even looking at each other. The Battleship totally ignored all three of us.

When the bell rang, I grabbed my things together and walked quickly out of the room, expecting the Battleship to call me back with every step. But she didn't say a word.

Which was almost scarier.

Out in the corridor, I clutched Hannah's arm. 'What happened?'

Her cheeks were pink. We started walking to history, pushing through the crowded hallways. 'Not much. She just made a big deal of comparing Tara's paper to mine, and said wasn't it interesting that we both missed the same problems. I told her that we always study together, that's all. She can't prove anything.'

My heart fell onto the floor. 'But you told her that *I* study with you too, right?'

'Oh, yeah, of course,' said Hannah quickly. Tara glanced at her, and didn't say anything.

'Listen, don't worry, she can't prove anything.' Hannah shook her hair back from her face. 'She's just a withered-up old crone; who would believe her?'

That Awful Industrial Powder

At lunch time I galloped home as usual, bursting through the door and racing up the stairs with hardly even a pause. Marcus barely looked up from the computer as I raced past.

Make up the beds, change the towels, clean the bathrooms. Marcus had really got his bit down pat, I had to give him that – the carpets were all clean, and the tea and coffee caddies had all been refilled. He probably had a scientific formula for doing them, so that he could get back to his beloved computer as fast as possible.

I leaned over the bathtub in Room Five, wiping it down. The cloth left a shiny trail in its wake.

'Could we have some clean towels, please?'

My skeleton almost leaped out of my skin as I whirled round. Mrs Dumont stood in the doorway behind me. Blimey, I hadn't even heard her come in! Her room had been the first one I'd done, and she hadn't been there then.

The bathtub's rim chilled my arm as I twisted to look at her. 'I've – I've already done your room.'

'Yes?'

'So – well, I mean, you already have clean towels.'

Her lips minced together as she shook her head. 'No, dear, the towels in our room are not what I would call clean.'

My cheeks blazed as I saw her take in my school uniform and raise her eyebrows. What was she even *doing* here? Guests always went out during the day! It was gorgeous outside!

'I'm sorry, I'll replace them,' I managed. But when I went to her room a few minutes later, she peered at the fresh towels in my arms and sighed.

'My dear, is this the best that we can do? Hmm?'

'They've just been washed—'

'With that awful industrial powder, no doubt. May I speak to your aunt, please?'

'My—'

'She *is* the one running things, isn't she?' Mrs Dumont squinted at me. Behind her, I could see her husband, lying on the bed reading a paper.

'Yes, of course,' I gasped. 'Only – she's doing the shopping now, so she's not here. And she's been a bit poorly, that's why I'm helping out. I'm sixteen,' I added, flinging it at her.

'I see,' was all she said. She gave me a smile that was more like a grimace, and took the towels from me. 'Well, tell her that I expect proper towels in future.'

The Rain in Spain

I was late back from lunch again that afternoon, but only by a minute or so, and I wasn't even the only one, for a change – Brian Vickery huffed into history a few seconds after I did.

I sat in the back with Hannah and Tara. Without even asking me, Hannah pulled her science homework out of her bag and edged it towards me, half-hiding it under my exercise book.

I looked down at it. It felt like my ribs were two sizes too small. Without meaning to, I glanced over at Milly, and flushed when I saw she was watching me. Her eyes flicked down to the paper on my desk, and she shrugged and turned away.

'Right, everyone!' At the front of the room, Mrs Hough clapped her hands. 'Let's have a geography quiz question to warm you up.'

'Are you sure I should?' I whispered to Hannah. 'I mean—'

Hannah shrugged. 'Well, not if you don't want to. Why, have you already done it?'

Oh, forget Milly! And forget the Battleship; she would have said something in class if she was going to turn us in. I pulled the paper towards me and started to copy.

'Ready?' said Mrs Hough. 'What's the principal

mountain range of Spain, bordering with France?'

My head came up as I looked at her, remembering the two oldies and their cycling trip in Spain.

'Come on, people. Mountain range in Spain . . .' Her eyes twinkled.

Hardly believing I was doing it, I raised my hand. Mrs Hough pointed at me. 'Sadie! Yes, what do you think?'

'It's the Pyrenees, miss.'

'Exactly right; good girl. Write that down, everyone – you never know; it just might be a bonus question on your next exam. Now, let's go over the reading from last night . . .'

Milly twisted round to look at me again, and gave me a smile with her eyebrows up, like – *Hey, not bad!*

Making up my mind suddenly, I pushed Hannah's paper back towards her. She and Tara were both staring at me. 'Um, here. I'll just – do it myself, and see how I get on.'

I'd Be Very Low-Key

'Hi, Mum.' I sat on the edge of her hospital bed, kissing her cheek. The sun was streaming in, angling across the bed. There was a vase of fresh daffodils from Tricia's florist shop on Mum's bedside table, and a couple of get-well cards.

She widened her eyes at me, smiling.

I rubbed her hand, feeling strangely happy all of the sudden. 'You know what I was remembering today? I was thinking about Dad's Hollywood Extravaganza nights.' That's what Dad used to call it when he'd rent old movies for us to watch. 'We used to make popcorn, remember?'

Mum blinked *yes*, keeping her eyes on mine.

'And remember when we watched *Gone with the Wind,* and at first you said it was too long to bother with? But then by the end we were both crying. And Dad pretended to be that actor, Clark something, and made us laugh.' I lowered my voice. '*Frankly, my dear* . . . remember?'

Mum's eyes shone softly, and I smiled, remembering. It was funny – we hardly ever talked about Dad at home, because Mum's face always went so stiff and sad when I tried to. But somehow everything had changed since she went into Intensive Care. I don't know how, but I knew that she wanted to hear about Dad as much as I wanted to talk about him.

'And do you remember when—'

'Sadie! Oh, good, you're here.' I turned around as Tricia came into the room, pulling up a chair and sitting beside me.

'How are you, Celia, all right?' Tricia leaned forward and squeezed Mum's arm with a smile before turning back to me. 'Sadie, I was with Celia for some time yesterday, and she spelled out a message for you

119

– at least, I assume it's for you. She wants to know where Leona is.'

The world stopped. I could feel Mum's eyes on me.

'She – she's at home,' I stammered. I didn't dare look at Mum.

Tricia took a piece of paper from her handbag. 'Here, I wrote it down. The full message is, *Where's Leona, it's been ages. Not this busy.* Which sounds like you don't think Leona is really too busy to see you, is that right, Celia?'

Yes, from Mum.

Heat prickled across my face. Hadn't Aunt Leona rung, then? She had promised! 'Um – well, the thing is, I guess she's still sort of upset about having to run Grace's. I mean, she's got *loads* better at it, and everything's going really well, but – but I don't think she wants to come see you yet.'

I risked a glance at Mum. Her mouth was turned down slightly, her eyes thoughtful.

No, she blinked.

'What do you mean?' My heart pounded in my chest like a caged tiger trying to escape.

No.

'Mum, it's true!' I whirled in my seat to look at Tricia. 'Tricia, honestly, that's all there is to it. There's nothing – nothing *bad* going on; everything's fine.'

Tricia stroked Mum's hand. 'Celia, would you like me to go and check, and meet this sister of yours?'

Yes.

'You can't!' I blurted out. 'I mean – I mean, Mum,

you know what Aunt Leona's like – she'll get in a huge strop if you send someone to check up on her!'

'Oh, I'd be very low-key,' put in Tricia.

I kept my eyes on Mum's face. 'Mum, please! I'll try to get her to come and see you, but you know what she's like – just let her get on with things in her own way, you know that's the best thing.'

We stared at each other for a long moment. Finally, Mum blinked *yes* again.

Tricia leaned forward. 'Celia, is that yes, you agree with Sadie? Or yes, you'd like me to go and check? Blink if it's the first one.'

Yes, blinked Mum.

I let out a breath, and fell back into my seat.

'Well, we'll leave it for now.' Tricia put the piece of paper back in her handbag. 'But Celia, let me know if you change your mind.'

Message from the Beach

Please pick up! Please, please! I sat on my bed gripping the cordless extension as Aunt Leona's mobile buzzed in my ear. At least it was ringing this time. And ringing. It felt like each ring was etching itself on my skull.

I held the phone to my ear and stared down at my duvet cover. It was cream-coloured, with bright red swirls on it.

'Hello?' Aunt Leona's voice was faint and crackly.

I sat bolt upright. 'It's me, Sadie!'

'Sadie! Hi, how are you? Ron and I just got back from snorkelling. It's so *amazing* here; there's this crystal-clear water, and—'

I clutched the phone. 'Aunt Leona, I've been trying to ring you! Did you ring Mum?'

Her voice faded in and out of static. 'Oh, Sadie, I tried – I rang the hospital like I said, but they said that she couldn't talk on the phone easily, and would I leave a message for her, so then I thought I'd better have a think about exactly what to say, so I told them I'd ring back, and—'

'Yes, but *did* you?'

'Well—'

'Because she's asking where you are! She's going to send someone round to check!'

Aunt Leona's voice faded for a moment, and then came back. '. . . someone to check? Who, for God's sake?'

'This woman, this GBS volunteer – Aunt Leona, you have to come home!'

'I can't, I've told you! My flight's not for another week and a bit. But Sadie, you have to keep holding the fort, OK?'

I wrenched the duvet cover between my fingers as wetness stung at my eyes. 'I have been! But I'm about to be found out, I know it, and I don't know what that will do to Mum—'

'*Do* to her? What do you mean?'

'You can die from GBS, if there're complications! And if I'm caught here, you could be arrested, and I'd be put in care, and—'

Aunt Leona's voice grew high-pitched, competing with the static. 'Sadie, you can't let anyone know! Because I could get in loads of trouble, and it wasn't my fault, really—'

'Oh, wasn't it!'

'No! I mean, I shouldn't have come here, but I *realized* that, only it was too late!'

Too late. Everything crashed together in my mind. The Battleship, Mum. How totally empty the flat was. I hugged myself, words choking to dust in my throat.

Aunt Leona took a breath. 'Look, I'll try ringing Celia again, OK? I'll do it now – I'll leave a message for her; I'll make up some reason why I haven't been to the hospital. Don't worry, Sadie, it'll all be OK. Only whatever you do, *you can't let anyone know.*'

I hung up slowly, the conversation spinning in my brain. And wondered what Mum would think when Aunt Leona *rang* instead of turning up.

I felt so stupid. I could have put on my Aunt Leona voice and left a message for Mum days ago. I hadn't even thought of that. Mum would never have been suspicious at all.

But now she was.

Lizard Eyes

The next morning, Mrs Dumont sent her breakfast back twice because my 'aunt' hadn't done her eggs to perfection. By the time she started saying things like, 'I've *never* stayed in a place with such appalling service!' Mr and Mrs Chambers were glaring at her. They were the only guests left in the dining room by then, and had made a special point the day before of telling me how much they'd enjoyed the Coast Path.

'I'm sorry – I'll take them back again,' I said, gritting my teeth.

'Oh, don't bother!' Mrs Dumont put her hands on the plate so I couldn't take it away. 'We've wasted enough time on this.'

Mr Dumont hadn't said a word all this time. He was busy keeping his head down, eating his imperfect eggs.

After all that I was almost late to school. I ran into the courtyard just after the first bell went, with everyone drifting into the school in a river of blue uniforms. I pressed into the crowd, breathing hard.

'Sadie, could I see you for a moment?' Vampira stepped out of her office the moment I walked in.

My blood turned to splinters of ice. Oh God, I should have known the Battleship wouldn't let it drop! I looked quickly around for Hannah and Tara, but didn't see them. Not that they could have helped me anyway.

Swallowing, I followed Vampira into her office. Mrs Clark gave me a bottomless look as I passed, like, *This is it for you, kiddo.*

'Have a seat.' Vampira closed the door behind me, and motioned to one of the blue-cushioned chairs in front of her desk. I sat stiffly, and tried to unclench my hands.

She sat across from me, her eyes dark and probing. 'Sadie, I'd like you to have a look at this.'

Just as I had expected, she handed me my maths paper from yesterday. The Battleship had marked it in red, lines slashing across two of the problems. I licked my lips, staring down at it like I had never seen it before.

'Is this your own work?'

My mind raced. What had the Battleship told her? I nodded quickly. 'Yes, miss. I mean, my friend Hannah helped me a bit, but—'

'I've spoken to Hannah,' she broke in. 'I had a word with both her and Tara Bishop yesterday. Hannah tells me that she and Tara do their work together, and that you often copy off them when you think they're not looking.'

Dryness swept my mouth. 'She – she said what?'

Vampira looked back at me impassively. 'That you copy off her and Tara. And that she's often tried to stop you, but you won't listen to her.'

I stared at her. I couldn't say anything. The lying cow!

She sat back in her chair, crossing her legs. 'Mrs

Shipton tells me that your work has improved rather dramatically, these last two weeks.'

Flames sizzled my face. I stared at her desk, not lifting my eyes. She had a little vase of dried flowers on it, and a shiny black stapler. Don't tell Mum. Oh, please don't tell Mum.

'Your other teachers say the same thing.'

I struggled to get the words out. 'I— I've just been really trying, that's all. Applying myself more.'

Her voice sounded almost gentle. 'Sadie, when you cheat you're only hurting yourself, you know.'

Well, why are *you* so bothered, then? I looked down at my shoes, and didn't say anything.

Vampira turned brisk again. 'We're also very concerned about your attendance since your mum went into hospital. You've been late to school twice, late back from lunch eight times, and absent once.'

My head snapped up. 'But my aunt rang to tell you about that!'

'Only about your absence and one of your latenesses. The rest were unexcused.' Vampira shook her head. 'Now, I know it's almost the end of term, Sadie, but we're still very concerned, especially with your mum ill.'

I licked my lips, wondering what she was getting at.

And then she got to it. 'I need to meet up with your aunt to have a chat.'

The floor dropped away from beneath my chair. Vampira's eyes were as motionless as a lizard's. 'We tried to ring her yesterday, and then again this morning, but we haven't been able to reach her.'

'No, she— she had to go to Dartmouth yesterday, I think. Um, and maybe again today.'

Something like an actual emotion flickered behind her eyes. 'Sadie, is everything all right at home?'

'Yes, everything's great! I mean, I've been worried about my mum, but – but yeah, everything's fine.'

She gazed at me for a long moment, and then picked up an envelope from a plastic tray on her desk. 'Give this to your aunt for me. Tell her it's urgent that I see her before the end of term on Friday.'

In slow motion, I watched my hand close around it. 'I will, but – but she's really busy—'

'Tell her that I *must* see her. I'll come to her if there's a problem,' said Vampira firmly.

No Offence

Our first class that day was English, with Mrs Green going on and on about Chaucer and *The Canterbury Tales*. I sat as far away from Hannah and Tara as I could, staring down at my book. The words churned on the page like bile. Mrs Green might have been babbling away in Latin for all I knew.

After the bell rang, Hannah and Tara caught up with me in the hallway.

'Sadie, did Vampira talk to you?' Hannah's eyes were wide and worried.

I kept striding down the hallway, and didn't answer.

They hurried to keep up with me. Hannah's throat moved as she swallowed. 'Um – what did you tell her?'

'Nothing,' I said coldly. 'So don't worry, the two of *you* are fine.'

Relief flooded Hannah's face. 'Oh, Sadie, thanks! You're a star, you really are.'

'Whatever.' I clutched the strap to my rucksack so tightly that my fingers throbbed. We went through the doors into the courtyard, heading towards the science block. I walked faster, but they didn't take the hint.

Hannah peered at me as we pressed through a group of Year Tens. 'You're not angry at us, are you?'

'Oh no, I'm thrilled! What do you think?' My voice shook.

She coloured. 'Sadie, I'm sorry, but – well, there was no point in *all* of us getting into trouble, was there? And you're more used to it than we are. No one expects you to do well.'

I stopped in my tracks and stared at her, and she smiled uncertainly. 'I mean . . . well, no offence.'

'Sadie, we're really sorry,' burst out Tara. 'We weren't trying to stitch you up—'

'No, it just sort of happened, right? Because we're such good friends, and I'm so thick anyway!' I pushed away from them and ran to our next class. When I got there, I sat in the back, holding a book open in front of me and ignoring them when they came in.

It wasn't too hard, since they seemed to be avoiding me, too.

Sort of Déjà-Vuey

I couldn't go home at lunch with Vampira on the prowl. I couldn't do anything except hide out in the girls' loos and cry. I went to the ones beside the gym because no one ever goes there at lunch, and just hugged myself and sobbed.

OK, fine – Hannah and I had never been fantastic friends, but at least I had thought we *were* friends. How could she do this to me, how? And now because of it, Vampira was going to come to my house. She'd know I'd been left on my own; I'd be taken into care. And Mum—

I gasped and leaned against one of the cold ceramic sinks, rubbing my eyes with a sodden wad of loo roll.

'Um . . . hi.'

I looked up. Milly stood in the doorway, looking as stricken as if she had caught me with no clothes on.

'What are you doing here?' I swiped at my face, throwing the loo paper in the bin.

She shrugged. 'Going to the loo?'

'Well, go on, don't let me stop you!'

Milly didn't move. 'This is sort of déjà-vuey, though,

isn't it? I mean, last time you *said* you had been crying in the loo, and now here you are . . .' She trailed off. 'Sorry. Just trying to make it into a joke.'

'Yes, it's just so extremely funny.' My eyes started leaking again, and I leaned into one of the cubicles to grab some more loo roll.

'Um, look . . . do you want to tell me what's wrong?'

'Why would I?' I blew my nose. In the mirror, my eyes looked like an albino rabbit's squinting back at me.

Milly shrugged. 'I don't know. Why not? A problem halved, and all that.'

Maybe she had a point. I sighed and looked down, staring at the cracks on the tiles. They made a sort of snowflake pattern. 'Milly . . . have you ever heard of Guillain-Barré Syndrome?'

She frowned, her grey eyes thoughtful. 'No, what's that?'

So I told her, all of it. Her eyes widened when I got to the part about Aunt Leona leaving.

'You are *joking*.'

'Yeah, I wish.'

'So what did you do?' She leaned against one of the sinks, staring at me.

I took a breath. 'I've been running Grace's on my own. That's why I've been late so often. And now Vampira wants to meet Aunt Leona, and—'

'Hang on.' Milly looked staggered. 'You've been running a B&B on your own?'

'Yeah.'

'For, like, two weeks now.'

'Yeah.'

'But that's *amazing*.'

I sighed. 'Milly, it's no big deal. You just make breakfast and make up their beds. Anyone could do it. It's just not getting caught.'

Her eyes flashed. 'Anyone could *not* bloody do it. I couldn't do it to save my life. God, I can't even make toast! And your aunt couldn't do it, could she?'

'Yeah, but she's useless,' I muttered.

'Well, you're certainly not.'

I stared at her, and she grinned. 'I mean, if I were stranded on a desert island, you'd be, like, the *perfect* person to have along. I bet you could make a shelter, and figure out a way to trap food, and—'

'I just couldn't get good marks,' I broke in.

'Who needs good marks on a desert island? This is real life.'

I held a towel from the dispenser under the cold tap, and wiped my face. 'Well, in *real life* I'll be taken into care unless I figure out a way to put Vampira off the scent. And Mum . . .' I swallowed, and couldn't finish.

Milly nodded. 'Don't worry, we'll figure something out.'

I looked at her. 'We?'

She smiled. 'Of course, *we*. We can't let you get taken into care; what if there's a desert island that needs sorting?'

I've Been Practising

So Milly came home from school with me that afternoon. I saw Hannah and the others staring as we walked down the front steps together, and I looked away, my jaw tightening. Milly didn't seem to notice, or didn't let on if she did.

'Oh, you live on this street!' She slowed down, looking at the sign for the beach and then up at the houses. 'Lucky you. It's like going back in time.'

'That's ours.' I pointed to Grace's.

'Really? God, I'd love to live in a place like that! You could pretend you were a princess or something.'

'I love it,' I said shyly. 'It was the house my dad grew up in.'

I didn't have to say he was dead. Everyone in my year already knew. Usually people's faces froze over if I mentioned him, like, *Oh no! What do we do now?* But Milly just nodded.

'That must be really nice. Like having a link with him all the time.'

My cheeks flushed. 'That's just how I feel.' Then I felt incredibly embarrassed, talking like that, and I didn't say anything else as we climbed up the drive.

'I'll have to make up the beds before we can talk,' I said as I put my key in the lock. 'They didn't get done at lunchtime.'

Milly followed me in, shutting the door behind her. 'That's OK; maybe I'll learn a useful skill.'

We went through the corridor and into the lounge. Marcus was there as usual, clicking away at the computer with a lock of his brown hair sticking up. I introduced him and Milly to each other.

'Cool website,' said Milly, looking over his shoulder.

He made a face. 'I have to sort out the reservations bit again . . . *she* made me take the old one off.'

I rolled my eyes. Yes, that's me, evil thwarter of small boys' websites. 'Whatever. We're going up to finish the rooms.'

A smirk crossed Marcus's face. 'What for?'

'What *for*? Er, because the beds need making up.' He just sat there, looking smug, and suddenly it twigged. 'You've already done them!'

His face reddened as he grinned. 'I've been practising.'

'Come on, show me!' We all ran to my room, and I ripped the covers off. Taking a deep breath, Marcus slowly, laboriously, made up the bed. And it wasn't *perfect* when he finished – there were a few little lumps and bumps here and there – but it was definitely a made-up bed.

'You did it!'

And even though it would have been seriously nice if he had figured this out two weeks ago, it was still pretty wonderful that he had finally got it, and I gave him a hug before I could stop myself.

He squirmed away, grimacing like I had the Black Death. '*Sa*-die . . . get off!'

Not Bad, Sherlock

Dear Miss Harris,

I am sorry to tell you that Sadie has been caught cheating recently, which appears to be an ongoing problem. I'm also concerned about her attendance of late. Please can you give me a ring as soon as possible to arrange a meeting so that we can discuss these issues before the end of term, and see whether there are any problems that we can help you to resolve.
Sincerely,
Samantha Bodley
Head of Year Nine, Drake Secondary School

'So,' said Milly, taking a swig of Coke. 'Points in our favour: you can imitate your aunt's voice, which is completely amazing, and Marcus can do the rooms by himself now, so you don't need to come home at lunch any more.'

Marcus smiled, and helped himself to a biscuit. We were all sitting out in the garden later that afternoon, with Vampira's letter on the wooden table between us. The sun beat down, warming the faded wood of the patio furniture as the raspy shriek of seagulls called around us.

I pushed my glass of Coke in a circle, following the ring of condensation. 'I thought of just ringing to say I couldn't make it – you know, as Aunt Leona. But Vampira said she'd come *here* if Aunt Leona didn't go in.'

'Let me think . . .' Milly leaned back in her deck chair, staring up at the silvery branches of our birch tree. I nibbled on a biscuit as I watched her.

'Right,' she said finally. 'Here's what you do. Today's Wednesday, so ring them up tomorrow, maybe from school somewhere if you can find a place to hide, and make an appointment for Aunt Leona to see Vampira on Friday. Then, on Friday, you don't go to school – you stay home, and ring them up as Leona again and say . . . oh, hang on, that wouldn't work.'

'What?' I hooked my ankles around the chair legs as I leaned forward. A salty breeze rustled past, lifting the hot air.

Milly shook her head. 'Well, I was going to say that you'd ring them up and say you're taking dear little Sadie up to Scotland for the summer, so sorry, you can't make the meeting, goodbye. Then it's the end of term, and that would be that. But I think you need an actual adult involved, somehow. Someone they can look at and say, *Ah-ha! Someone responsible!*'

'My mum!' said Marcus, sitting up.

I made a face at him. 'Marcus . . . how?'

He shrugged his narrow shoulders. 'I don't know.

She could take a note in, or something. She wouldn't have to know what's in it.'

Milly and I looked at each other. 'Actually . . .' I said.

Milly tapped the table. 'Hang on, hang on – if she didn't say anything, if she just dropped it off and left—'

'Then they'd think *she* was Aunt Leona!' The words bumbled over each other in my excitement. 'Especially if we put it in a sealed envelope, so that they didn't open it and ask questions straight away – Marcus could tell her that all she has to do is walk in and drop it off at Reception, that they're expecting it!'

Milly nodded slowly, her eyes shining. 'Not bad, Sherlock,' she said.

Locked in Hell

I was almost too scared to go and see Mum again, now that she was asking about Aunt Leona . . . but I had to. I couldn't just leave her lying there, all alone. That afternoon I walked into her room like a rabbit heading into a trap – and then relaxed when I saw that thankfully, thankfully, Tricia wasn't there.

'Hi, Mum.' I sat down next to her. Her brown eyes moved over to mine. They looked dull, like unpolished wood, and I swallowed.

'How – how are you feeling?'

No response. Not a flicker, not a flutter.

I fiddled with a shell bracelet that Dad had given me. 'School's almost finished for the term. Just two more days.'

Her gaze drifted to the window. And suddenly I realized how much she had managed to say to me without saying a word, this last week or so. Because now she was gone.

My voice cracked. 'Um . . . Aunt Leona says that when I'm out of school, I can help out more at Grace's . . .' I trailed off. Mum was still looking away, not moving, not smiling, not anything.

'Mum, I'll— I'll be right back.' I gripped her hand for a second, and then rushed out of the room.

I found Brenda at the nurse's station, filling out a form. She looked up when she saw me. 'Sadie, what's wrong?'

'It's Mum, she—' I struggled to speak.

She leaped up like a greyhound about to burst from the gate. 'What? Is the ventilator still working?'

'Yes! It's nothing like that, she just—' I pressed my lips together.

Brenda paused, looking at me. 'Sadie?'

'She just . . . doesn't seem very happy to see me.' Tears threatened, and I jerked my head away, staring at a blood donation poster on the wall. It sounded so daft once I said it, as though Mum should be doing cheers every time I walked in the door!

Brenda sighed, her eyes softening. 'Oh, Sadie . . . come here, let's talk for a minute.' She took me over to the waiting area, and we sat down on a pair of horrid green plastic chairs. 'Listen, your mum's reaction is nothing personal, OK?'

I wiped my eyes. 'OK.'

She touched my arm. 'No, honestly. The thing is, patients with GBS can often feel very depressed. I mean, think about it – she's trapped in there, she can't move or talk, she doesn't know what's going on.'

Her words echoed like stones dropped in a well. I hadn't really thought much about what it must be like for Mum, locked in her body. Once I did, I couldn't stop.

It must be like hell on earth.

Brenda kept talking. 'We do our best to keep her stimulated, but obviously it's a very difficult time for her. She loves seeing you, though.'

I stared at her. 'She does?'

'Yes, she does. She always seems much more cheerful after you've been.' Brenda glanced at her watch, and stood up. 'Sadie, I have to get back to work. You should have a word with Tricia though; she's in most days. She can tell you what it's like.'

No thanks; that was just the person I was trying to avoid.

Brenda squeezed my shoulder and walked away, her steps trim and brisk. I took a shaky breath and went back into Mum's room. She hadn't moved, of course, and lay exactly where she had been, still gazing out the window. I sat down and took her hand, and her head moved listlessly towards me.

I didn't say anything for ages, just sat there and

held her hand. Her fingers felt cool, with no movement at all to them.

And we just looked at each other. It was like I was seeing her for the first time.

'It'll be OK, Mum,' I whispered finally, brushing her hair back from her forehead. 'It'll be OK.'

An Original Feature

I stayed up for ages on Thursday night, making sure that we had enough clean sheets and duvet covers for the hen party coming the next day. Because when someone checked out, I had to *totally* remake the bed, with everything completely clean, and everyone who was staying with us was checking out in the morning.

Including the Dumonts, thank God.

Ever since they had checked in, I had thought about taking the special offer sign down and burning it or something, because if *they* were the sort of customers it brought in, I seriously did not want any more.

Just the night before, Mrs Dumont had knocked on the lounge door, asking whether we had a hot water bottle. In July.

'Um, I'm not sure . . .'

Her nostrils twitched. 'Well, can you ask? There's a definite chill coming in through our window. You don't have double glazing here.'

No, because the sash windows were an original feature of the house, and my dad would have slit his wrists with a rusty bread knife before he tore them out and replaced them with plastic rubbish.

I didn't say that. I just smiled and said, 'I'll ask.' I shut the door in her face and went over to Mum's bedroom door, calling, 'Aunt Leona! Have we got a hot-water bottle?'

And we didn't, but I got the electric blanket down from the shelf in Mum's wardrobe and took it back to the door. 'Sorry, we can't find one, but she says you can use this.'

Mrs Dumont sort of huffed. 'You mean I have to re-do the bed?'

'I'll come and do it—'

She grabbed the blanket from me. 'No, that's all right; I'll do it myself!'

And so on. Every time I saw her, she had a look on her face as though she could smell rotting fish. Couldn't my aunt do this or that, and *other* B&Bs gave customers discount coupons for restaurants in town, and blah blah blah. I was terrified that she was going to insist on speaking to Aunt Leona if she didn't get her way, and I leaped to do everything she said.

So I wasn't exactly heartbroken that they were checking out. I reckoned having a whole hen party staying with us would be child's play compared to her.

Marcus Knows How to Cross the Street

Dear Miss Bodley,

I'm extremely sorry, but I won't be able to meet with you today as planned. Sadie is very unhappy here with her mother in hospital, and so I've decided to take her up to Scotland to see her grandmother for a few weeks, to cheer her up. (I'm sorry that she'll miss the last day of term, but if school is anything like it was in my day, not much will have been going on anyway!)

Let me assure you that everything is all right, and that I'm sure Sadie will start the new term in September feeling refreshed and ready to go.

Yours sincerely,
Leona Harris

Milly and I had spent hours on the letter – she wrote it on the computer, and then I forged Aunt Leona's signature. I thought it was a complete work of genius. I mean, it didn't sound the least bit like Aunt Leona, but it was so perfectly *adult.*

Even so, I could hardly concentrate as I did the breakfasts on Friday morning. I served everyone automatically, keeping a big smile on my face, but inside I felt like a jar lid that's been twisted on too tight. What if our plan didn't work?

Mrs Dumont was the last guest down. She sat by herself beside the window, looking grim. 'My husband isn't feeling well this morning.' She snapped her napkin open on her lap, eyeing me like it was my fault. 'So please hurry with my breakfast, so I can get back to him.'

'I'm sorry Mr Dumont's ill,' I said as I took in her breakfast ten minutes later.

'Yes, it's probably something he ate.' She poked at her eggs with a fork, scowling.

I'm sure it's nothing to do with *stress*. I went back into the kitchen. At least that was everyone finished with breakfast for now.

Which meant that it was time.

My hands trembled slightly as I carefully folded the letter up, putting it in a plain white envelope and sealing it. *For Miss Bodley*, I wrote on the front, using my left hand and writing in a quick, adult scrawl.

Then I took a deep breath and rang Mrs Marcus.

'What's your surname?' I hissed at Marcus as the phone rang.

He adjusted his glasses. 'Bowers.'

That's right, Bowers. Thankfully, Marcus's mum answered the phone before I could forget it again.

'Hello, Mrs Bowers?' I said in my Aunt Leona voice.

'Yes?'

'This is Leona Harris, from next door—'

'Oh, hello!' Her voice warmed. 'I'm so glad to speak to you at last— you must think I'm awful, not coming round sooner! I did try a few times— in fact, I was going to pop over a few nights ago, but Marcus said you were probably too busy.'

Thank you, Marcus. I tried to laugh. 'Yes, we do keep pretty busy here.'

'I suppose you're ringing because it's the last day of his project?'

I had forgotten all about that. I glanced at Marcus. 'Oh – yes, I just wanted to say that— that he's done a great job, and been a big help, actually—'

'Well, he's been *very* keen about learning all he can these last couple of weeks, and it's been really good of you to have him there. We've been combining all sorts of fun lessons with it in the evenings – maths, and history, and English—'

She gushed on for ages, and I felt pretty sorry for Marcus by the end of it. Finally I was able to clear my throat and break in. 'I was just wondering, do you think you might be going out today?'

'Out?'

'Yes, I— you see, there's a form for Sadie's school that she was meant to take in with her, but she's forgotten it, and I think they need it this morning. I have to stay here and do the rooms, but Marcus said you might—'

'Oh.' She sounded taken aback. 'Well, Marcus could drop it off for you. It's only two streets away.'

No! My heart jammed my throat as I clutched the phone. 'Oh, I don't think so – I mean, the streets are so busy around the school—'

She laughed. 'They're not that busy. And Marcus knows how to cross the street; he'll be fine.'

I stared at Marcus across the kitchen. '*What? What?*' he was mouthing. Utter doom, that's what.

'All right. Thank you, I'll have him take it,' I said finally.

'Yes, he'll be fine. And thank *you* for being so good about his project!'

Click.

'What now?' I banged the phone down and slumped against the counter, hugging my elbows. 'She won't do it, she says *you* can drop it off!'

Marcus perked up. 'OK!'

'It is not OK. We have to have an adult do it! If they see you instead, they'll ask loads of questions; it'll ruin everything!'

His eyes glowed behind his glasses. 'But no one would see me, I promise! I'd choose my moment *really carefully*, and sneak in and—'

I gripped my temples, trying to think. Could I get one of the guests to do it, maybe? Tell them it was my little sister who went to school there? No, it would look too weird; they'd wonder why I couldn't take it.

I bit my lip, and looked at Marcus.

He stood on tiptoes, almost trembling, like a dog who'd heard the word *walkies*. 'Please! I won't get caught, I promise! I'll just sneak in and put it on the desk!'

There was no one else.

Slowly, I watched myself hand him the letter. 'Marcus, listen to me. This is so important. If you're caught—' I stopped. 'Just – don't be caught.'

I Think You'll Find

I couldn't stand listening to the silence after he left. I put a Robbie Williams CD on and did the dishes, dreading with every swipe of the sponge that the phone would ring, and it would be Vampira announcing she was on her way over.

After half an hour, I had dried all the dishes and put them back in the cupboard, and there was still no sign of Marcus. Where was he? The school was only about two seconds away! I imagined him tied up in Vampira's office, refusing to speak while she tortured him.

One by one, I heard the guests leaving, putting their keys on the hall table. Finally it was half-nine, and I thought my brains were going to leak out of my ears. What was going on? Had he been caught, or what?

I grabbed up the pile of fresh sheets and duvet covers and went upstairs. I might as well get the rooms done for the hen party while I died of anxiety. Dumping the clean laundry on the first-floor landing, I went from room to room, stripping all the beds.

Then I opened the door to Room Seven, and my heart jammed into my throat.

'Oh!' I started, jumping backwards. 'Oh, I'm sorry—'

Mrs Dumont was sitting in the armchair drinking a cup of tea, and Mr Dumont was lying in bed reading a paper. She narrowed her eyes at me. 'Yes?'

'I'm sorry – it's just that it's almost checkout time; I thought you'd gone—'

She sipped her tea. 'I forgot to tell you; we're going to stay over tonight, as well. And possibly tomorrow night, depending on how my husband's feeling.'

The key gouged into my palm. 'I'm— I'm really sorry, but you can't.'

She stared at me, unblinking. In the bed, Mr Dumont turned a page of his paper.

'I mean – we're completely full tonight. We don't have any rooms left.'

Mrs Dumont very carefully put her teacup down. 'Yes, but my husband is ill.'

A cavern opened up in my stomach. 'I'm sorry, I really am, but we just don't have any rooms. I could ring another B&B for you—'

You know how in horror films, monsters can just *whoosh* straight at you? That's what it was like. One second she was sitting in the soft cream-coloured armchair, and the next she was right in front of me, staring up into my face with hard, glinty eyes.

'Shall we step outside?' she said pleasantly. 'I'd prefer not to disturb my husband.'

I swallowed, and went out into the corridor. Mrs Dumont followed, closing the door.

'Now, *you listen to me*,' she hissed, planting herself in front of me. 'My husband is ill with some sort of stomach upset, and for all I know he got it from the cooking here! I'm not moving him until he's feeling better, and I think you'll find that the law is on our side.'

She spun on her heel and went back into the room. *Bang*. The door closed in my face.

'All right, darling?' A male voice. My God, he talked!

'Yes, fine. Go back to sleep, dear.'

I stumbled through the rest of the guest rooms in a haze, tugging sheets and duvet covers off. My fingers had turned as clumsy as Marcus's. What was I supposed to do now? The hen party had already paid to stay here; they'd be furious when they didn't have all of their rooms!

They'd demand to speak to someone in charge . . .

My head jerked up as I heard the faint echo of a door banging shut. I pelted downstairs, almost losing my footing on the landing, and exploded into our flat.

Marcus was sitting at the computer, booting it up. He started backwards on the seat when I burst in.

'Where have you *been*?' I shouted. 'What happened?'

His eyes widened. 'Nothing! I just had to hang about outside until the woman at the desk went away for a few seconds, that's all. Then I snuck in and put it on her desk and left.'

'Did anyone see you?'

He shook his head.

'Oh, thank God! I was getting so worried—' I collapsed onto the sofa and tried to calm down, pushing my hands through my hair.

Marcus stared at me. 'Sadie . . . is anything wrong?'

A laugh like you might hear on a mental ward escaped me. 'Yes, Marcus. Yes, you could say that.'

I looked past him at the door to Mum's room. And I knew that I didn't have any choice.

A Real Girly Slumber Party

Dad said once that a guest room wasn't really a bedroom; it was more like an ideal of a bedroom – because they look so gorgeous and perfect, as if no one's ever set foot in them before. Real bedrooms, he said, were completely different and no one would ever want to stay in them, which was why people liked leaving their own bedrooms once in a while and going somewhere else.

Once Marcus and I had cleared Mum's room out, I saw exactly what Dad had meant. The carpet looked flat and grubby. There was a scratch on the front of the wardrobe. A white ring on the bedside table where she had put a glass of water.

It was a mess even though it was totally empty.

'We're never going to get away with this,' I whispered.

Marcus shoved damp hair back, staring around him. 'What's wrong with it?'

'What's *wrong* with it? Are you mad? It needs new paint, new furniture, new . . .' I trailed off, staring around me. 'No one will want to stay here; it looks totally knackered! They're going to want to speak to Aunt Leona when they see this—'

The phone on Mum's bedside table rang.

A bath bomb of panic hit my stomach. What if it was school, checking up on me? I clutched my elbows as it rang and rang, like a headache that wouldn't go away.

Then I heard the machine in the lounge pick up, and a bright female voice said, 'Oh, hi, this is Kathy Marks – I'm the bridesmaid who's organizing the hen party tonight—'

I hesitated, feeling ill. Finally, slowly, I picked up the phone.

'Hello, this is Grace's – sorry, I didn't get to the phone in time.'

Kathy laughed as the machine beeped, turning itself off. 'Oh, that's OK! Is that Celia?'

I twisted the cord around my hand. 'No, this is Leona, her sister. Celia – Celia's away right now, so I'm running Grace's for her.'

'Oh, right. Off on holiday, eh?' She laughed again. 'Listen, I was just ringing to check that everything's OK for tonight.'

I looked around me at the faded wallpaper, the

scruffy carpet. 'I – um, there's a bit of a problem, actually.'

'Oh, what?'

'Well – there's a guest who was supposed to be checking out today, but he's ill, and can't be moved . . . so we're, we're . . . sort of short of a room.' My throat had turned to cold lead.

'Oh, no! Well, listen, I'm sure we can sort something out – we had a couple of the girls in singles, so two of them can just double up.'

It took me a second to realize that she was saying it was OK. That she wasn't going to call the police and press charges against us. When I did realize it, I was so relieved that I almost forgot to sound like Aunt Leona. 'Really? Are you sure it's all right?'

'Oh, sure. It'll be more fun that way, anyway. We can have a real girly slumber party.' She giggled.

'Thank you so much! I'll give you the money back for the room—'

'Yeah, we'll work it out. These things happen. Listen, I'll be getting there around four or so, so if you have the keys ready, I can just hand them out to everyone, so you don't have to hang about.'

'Oh, that's fine!' I said, smiling. 'And by the way, my sixteen-year-old niece Sadie is here, helping out. You'll probably be seeing a lot of her.'

Kathy laughed again. 'Great! She can join the party.'

Paint the Town Red

By six o'clock, Grace's sounded like a girls' dormitory at a boarding school. I sat in our lounge trying to watch TV, but I could hardly even hear it. You'd think that people who had to be at least thirty would be a bit more mature, but the house teemed with shrieks and laughter and high heels pounding up and down the stairs.

'Becky! I haven't seen you in ages!'

'Heather, you're looking fabulous!'

'Right, is that everybody? Who's not here?' I heard Kathy raise her voice over the crowd in the front hallway. When she checked in earlier, she had looked exactly as I'd pictured – short black hair and a pixie-ish face.

'Sam's not here,' called someone.

'Oh, right, Sam . . . God, and she's local! No excuse! Right, hang on . . .' A pause, and then, 'Sam! Where are you? You're not still at work, you big girly swot? Just because you're this form head hotshot now doesn't mean – oh, good. She's almost here now,' called Kathy to the others.

'You'd better be talking on a hands-free, you naughty girl!' shrieked a voice.

Kathy said something else, but I didn't hear it. I was sitting bolt-upright by then, staring at the closed door between our lounge and the hallway.

A form head hotshot.

No. No way, it couldn't be. Fate could not have such a sick sense of humour.

Feeling like I was walking underwater, I went over to the dining table, where Vampira's letter had been last seen. At first I couldn't find it, and I spent a few pointless minutes shuffling through flyers for pizza and stuff like that. Then I spotted a piece of paper lying on the floor, and ducked down to pick it up.

Samantha Bodley, Head of Year Nine. Sam.

My skin turned clammy. OK, calm down, this didn't mean anything! Samantha was a hugely common name. Just because this particular Sam was local, and was a form head, didn't mean—

I stiffened as I heard the popping-gravel sound of a car pulling into our car park. Edging over to the window, I plucked the curtain aside the barest inch, squinting outside.

An electric-blue Toyota was parked in our lot with its boot gaping open, and a slim, dark-haired woman was leaning into it, wearing faded jeans. My spine relaxed. Vampira would *not* wear jeans. It would be like the Queen shopping at The Gap.

The woman straightened up and swung an overnight bag over her shoulder, slamming the boot shut. I sucked in a breath, and dropped the curtain like it was scorching my hand. No! This couldn't be true, it couldn't be happening!

The doorbell rang, and a shrieking stampede raced to open it.

'Sam! You're here!'

'Sam, it's been ages since I've seen you!'

And then Vampira's voice, which hardly sounded like her voice at all. 'Hello, you lot! Here to paint the town red, are we?'

I pressed tightly against the lounge door, my pulse crashing at my temples. Maybe I was hallucinating? But no, it was her.

'Sorry I'm late, everyone,' I heard her say. 'Our school secretary was ill today, and we had a hopeless temp – it was complete end-of-term chaos—'

'Leave it at work, you workaholic!' laughed Kathy. 'Come on, here's your key – now, let's go tart ourselves up and hit the nightspots of Brixham!'

'Yeah, all two of them!' called someone else, and the voices moved upstairs, laughing and chattering.

Holding my head, I sank to the floor like my knees had turned to seaweed. Vampira, staying in my house.

I was dead.

Life in the Real World

'Right, calm down,' said Milly. 'This is *not* the end of the world.'

'Then tell me what is!' I paced back and forth across the lounge, clutching the phone to my ear.

I could just picture her giving me that half-smile

of hers. 'Um, nuclear war? Famine? Come on, we can handle this.'

'How? Tell me how!'

'They're all checking out tomorrow, right? So it's simple; she just can't see you.'

'Then how am I going to serve them breakfast?' My voice bounced around the room.

'Well, I could come and help. Get in a bit of domestic service practice.'

'No, she *knows* you. It would look too weird; she'd be suspicious . . . it has to be an adult.' I sank down onto the sofa, gripping the phone so hard that my knuckles hurt.

'OK, let's think. Who do we know that—?'

'Milly, there isn't anyone. If I knew an adult who could serve breakfast to people and keep a big secret, I wouldn't be in this mess in the first place!'

The doorbell rang. I ignored it. The hen party had left half an hour ago to descend upon Brixham, and if someone was looking for a room, they were out of luck.

I threw myself back against the sofa. 'Well, go on, then. Do *you* have a handy spare adult about who can magically save the day?'

There was a long pause. I could practically hear the cogs in Milly's brain whirring away. 'Um, no, actually,' she said finally. 'My sister would have done it, but she's at uni up in Newcastle.'

'Very helpful.'

'What about—?'

The doorbell rang again, longer this time. And just in case I hadn't got the hint, the letterbox snapped open and shut a few times. 'Hello?' called a man's voice.

I groaned, and sat up. 'Milly, I'll have to ring you back, OK? Someone's at the door.'

'Right, well, don't give up meanwhile. We'll think of something!'

Riinng. 'I'm coming,' I muttered. I swung open the front door, and a tiny white-haired couple smiled up at me.

'Oh, hello! This is Grace's Place, isn't it?' asked the man.

'Yes, but—'

He beamed. 'We were afraid we had the wrong one! I'm John Brochu, and this is my wife Helene.'

Faint, unpleasant bells rang. I stared at him, trying to remember.

'We booked a room for three nights through your website. Actually, our grandson did it for us – I hope it worked?'

Mrs Brochu gave a little flutter, and dipped into her black leather handbag. 'Oh! Here, we have a confirmation number.'

She held out a piece of paper in her soft, creased hand. I gazed down at it. It was as though I had forgotten how to read.

'Right,' I heard myself say finally. 'Yes, right, we were expecting you.' I moved aside so they could come in, and a single, weary thought flickered through my mind: *Marcus, I am going to rip the hard drive out of our*

155

computer and bash you over the head with it.

I tried to smile. 'Sorry, my aunt is running things, and she's out at the moment.'

Mr Brochu's eyes twinkled. They really did, like the sun glistening on the bay. 'Well, we're later than expected. Shall we go and have dinner in town until she's back?'

'No,' I said distantly. 'No, that's OK, I can check you in. Only, the thing is—'

I gulped – suddenly, stupidly, near tears. For a completely mad moment, I wanted to tell this sweet old couple everything, *everything*, and then maybe they'd decide to be my grandparents and swoop in and save the day.

Yeah, right. Try life in the real world, Sadie.

I took a breath. 'Nothing. If you want to go and get your bags, I'll have your room ready in a moment.'

So I put them in Mum's room.

I had a quick tidy of our lounge while they were getting their things – which I kept pretty tidy anyway, because I can't stand having a mess around me – and banged the French doors leading to the kitchen shut. I had just put a lace placemat on Mum's bedside table, hiding the water stain, when I heard them come in again.

'Hi, um – it's this way.'

They blinked when I led them into the lounge. 'Is this a newer section of the house?' asked Mr Brochu.

'No, it's the same age as the rest of it.' I chewed on a nail. My dad had always *meant* to rip out the horrible seventies fireplace and replace the carpet with something that didn't look like it belonged in a pub, but then he'd think of some other fantastic thing he could do upstairs, and go and do that instead. It used to drive Mum spare.

'It's our largest room, actually,' I said, clearing my throat. 'See, it has its own sitting area here. And it's an en-suite.' I opened up the door to Mum's bedroom, and showed them her loo.

The Brochus looked at each other, and I knew they were about to complain. To refuse to sleep in what was obviously someone's real bedroom, or sit in what was obviously someone's run-down lounge. They'd throw a strop and demand to speak to Aunt Leona, and you know what? I hardly even cared any more.

'Thank you,' said Mrs Brochu finally. 'It's lovely.'

Dad

I dreamed about my dad that night.

Just after he died, I used to dream about him all the time. Really ordinary dreams – he'd be out working in the garden, maybe, or painting a chair. And we'd just be talking, him asking about my day and what I had been doing.

I hadn't had one of those dreams in years, and I

really missed them. So even in my dream, I was all excited about seeing him again. We were standing on Breakwater Beach, skipping stones, and I said, *Dad! I can't believe you're here!*

He grinned at me, and spun a stone so that it skimmed across the water like a flying fish. *Of course I'm here,* he said. *I'm always here.* I could see Grace's over his shoulder, shining whitely in the sunshine.

That was it; it wasn't a long dream. But when I woke up I felt like I had been given a chest full of glittering rubies and diamonds. I had seen my dad again! His face, so clear – the laughter lines around his eyes, the crescent-shaped scar on his chin from where he crashed a motorbike when he was a teenager.

'Thanks, Dad,' I whispered, hugging myself and smiling. And suddenly everything seemed possible, even with Vampira sleeping somewhere upstairs.

I was *not* going to give up. Not now.

Favour to Humanity

'Sadie!' Mrs Marcus held her dressing gown closed with one hand. She wasn't wearing her round praying-mantis glasses, and her face looked raw without them. 'What brings you here so early?'

I shifted on her doorstep. The day already felt warm, even in my sleeveless T-shirt. 'I'm sorry to bother you, but – I sort of need your help.'

'Oh?' She frowned, and stepped back. 'Here, come in. What's wrong?'

Marcus's house was the same size as ours, but it looked like it was trying to be a library, with high wooden shelves crammed with dusty books every-where. Even the front hallway had a bookshelf in it.

'Um – it's my aunt. She's ill, she's been throwing up – she can't cook the breakfasts this morning, there's just no way. And I've never done them; I don't know what to do.'

Her pale eyes bulged slightly, like I had asked her to fling her robe off and dance the can-can. 'You want *me* to come and do them?'

I let my eyes fill with tears, which wasn't hard. 'Please, I don't know who else to ask! People are going to be downstairs wanting their breakfast any second now, and my mum will get into trouble if—'

Mrs Marcus winced. 'Yes, I see. I'll— I'll go and get changed.'

I could hear a computer game going somewhere in the house, so once she disappeared upstairs, I followed the noise, picking my way around piles of books on the floor. I couldn't believe the mess. No wonder Marcus hadn't known how to make a bed.

The noise was coming from a door beside the kitchen, which was full of plates with food caked on them, and teetering pots and pans beside the sink. I wrinkled my nose and opened the door – and found a room that looked like it might be a study, if you mucked out all the papers on the floor and fumigated it. And sure enough, there was the techno-genius himself, clicking away at a keyboard.

He jerked his head back when he saw me. 'Sadie! What are you doing here?'

I ducked under the desk and unplugged the computer, wriggling the plug out of the socket.

Marcus yelped as though I had ripped him off life support. 'What are you doing? That was *Battlestar Warriors*!'

'A favour to humanity! Because guess what – the *Brochus* checked in last night.'

Marcus had fallen straight to his knees, scrambling to plug the computer back in, and now his head peered up slowly over the desk. 'The Brochus?'

'Name sound familiar?'

He stood up, blinking rapidly. 'But I cancelled their reservation; they couldn't have!'

'Oh, silly me, they must be a hallucination. One that's staying in Mum's bedroom.'

'Well – well, at least you had a room for them, right . . . ?'

I could actually feel my nostrils flare as I glared at him. Thankfully for him, Mrs Marcus appeared in the doorway just then, wearing a pair of baggy trousers and a short-sleeved jumper.

'Sadie, are you ready?'

'Where are you going?' Marcus scrambled back up onto his chair.

She sighed, jingling her house keys in her hand. 'Sadie's aunt is ill, so I have to go help out at Grace's. You stay here – remember to start your interactive French programme at nine o'clock.'

Marcus's eyes widened as he looked at me.

'I'll tell you later,' I muttered as Mrs Marcus left the room. Because maybe he had done his best to ruin my life with his stupid website . . . but I suppose he was all right, really.

When It's Not Coming Out One End . . .

Now that school had finished I'd changed the times for breakfast again, so people could order until half-nine. The hen party had asked to have theirs served as late as possible, which didn't surprise me since it had been two o'clock in the morning before they rolled back to Grace's, singing some song about getting married in the morning. I imagined Vampira with a hangover, and shuddered.

'Does your aunt need anything?' asked Mrs Marcus as I opened the back door. We went into the kitchen, and she glanced at the closed French doors. 'Some dry toast, maybe, or—'

I shook my head. 'No, I think she's sleeping. When she's not being ill. She was up most of the night – she said when it wasn't coming out one end, it was coming out the other.'

Mrs Marcus paled. 'I see. Well, let's just let her sleep, then, shall we?' She read the list above the hob, and her eyes stretched wide behind her glasses. 'Good heavens. We have to cook all *this*?'

I frowned, wondering what she meant. 'Well, it's a Full English Breakfast.'

She bit her lip, not moving. I took out the frying pan and showed her where the spatula was, and she rubbed her palms on her trousers.

'Right, well . . . I suppose we start by asking everybody what they want?'

'I already know that.' I gave her the order sheets I had collected the night before, and glanced at the clock. Why wasn't she getting on with it? Everyone was probably already in there, waiting!

Mrs Marcus flicked through the sheets. 'Oh, that's a clever idea of your mum's. OK, right, so we know what each person wants . . . and let's see, they all want eggs, it looks like, so we'll need . . .'

'Here.' I handed her two cartons of eggs from the fridge, and two packs of bacon. 'This should be enough.'

She looked at them, her lips tight in concentration, and then stared back at the orders. 'OK, right. And hash browns . . . oh dear, how do you cook those? Do you have any potatoes?'

I stared at her. 'No, you cook them from frozen.' I took a pack out of the freezer and opened it. 'You can fry them, or just grill them while you do the bacon and sausage – that's probably faster; it's what I— what my mum usually does.'

It was like that for *everything on the list*. I even had to open up the can of baked beans for her, and stop her from dumping them in the frying pan with the eggs. I stood twitching to one side while she tried to cook, aching to just jump in and do it myself. Poor Marcus! No wonder he was so scrawny.

I cringed as she accidentally broke one of the egg yolks with the spatula. 'Um – you know, I think maybe I could do the cooking.'

'No, no, don't be silly,' she muttered, prodding at the streaming yellow river.

'Yes, but I think I know how. From watching my mum.'

She ignored me, and ruined a few more of the eggs. Finally I couldn't take it any more, and I edged in beside her, flipping the bacon over before it burned.

'There!' Mrs Marcus smiled triumphantly as she slipped an underdone egg onto a plate. 'That's the first two finished – if you take them in, I'll get the next two ready.'

The breath felt kicked out of me. 'No, *you* need to do that!' I blurted.

'Sadie, I'm busy cooking.'

'I'm underage; I'm not allowed! Please, you have to do it – my mum might really get in trouble otherwise.'

Mrs Marcus's mouth thinned, and she rolled her eyes a bit. 'All right, fine. Where's the dining room, in through there?'

She carried the plates out, and I sagged with relief. Then, while she was gone, I quickly turned the heat down on the grill and threw out the mess in the frying pan, cracking fresh eggs into it.

Timing

I thought it would get easier for her after that, but instead she got more and more flustered with each breakfast she did, until finally her hands were shaking and she looked near tears.

'Oh, this is hopeless!' Mrs Marcus jumped back as one of the sausages popped, hissing grease. 'It's the *timing* that's so impossible! How do you get everything to come out at the same time?'

The timing? But that wasn't even hard! 'Well, if you just . . .' I trailed off, realizing that I didn't know how to explain it. The timing just happened, that was all.

Mrs Marcus stabbed the sausages onto two more plates, and thrust them at me. 'Here, take these in.'

'But—'

Her hair clung to her forehead as she sliced more mushrooms. 'Go on! Silly girl, no one's going to report you.'

I gripped the plates hard enough to shatter them. 'No, really, my mum would get into trouble—'

'Sadie!' She spun towards me. 'I'm going to lose patience in a moment! Just take the plates out.'

I stared at the door. 'Is it . . . still the hen night out there?'

'Yes, and half of them don't have their breakfast! *Honestly*, Sadie, what's wrong with you?'

I swallowed. I had to either tell her, or go.

So I went.

Every step I took felt like a knife gouging into my chest. I shook my head frantically as I walked down the corridor, so that my hair would cover my face. My blonde, impossible-to-miss hair!

My nerves screamed as I backed into the dining room, keeping my head down. Glancing up under my hair, I could see Vampira sitting with three other women at Table Six, clutching her forehead as she took a sip of coffee. She already had a plate of food in front of her, even if it looked like she had hardly touched it.

Kathy sat at Table Three, looking just as miserable. Turning quickly away from Vampira, I set the plates down in front of her and the plump brown-haired woman beside her. 'Here you go,' I smiled.

'Oh, thank you, Sadie,' she moaned, and I stiffened. Don't look at Vampira, don't check to see if she's heard!

'Could we just have a bit more coffee?' asked Kathy.

Casual, act casual. I lowered my voice. 'Yes, sure.' I went to the sideboard, trying to keep my face turned away from Vampira without looking like I had a crick in my neck.

'Ohh, my head feels like it's gone swimming,' said

165

Kathy as I poured the coffee.

'Well, um – enjoy your breakfast.' I couldn't stop myself; I glanced over at Vampira again. She was leaning on her hand, talking to the woman next to her.

Just as I was about to slip out the door, a voice said, 'Wait just a moment, please.'

Food for Thought

I stiffened as though a bullet had whistled past my ear. I hadn't even noticed Mrs Dumont, but there she was, sitting in the corner and looking like she had just swallowed a peppercorn. 'I'd like to register a complaint about the noise last night,' she announced.

'The noise?' I glanced over my shoulder, and then back at her, swallowing.

'Yes, the noise. We were awakened in the middle of the night by singing and shouting, and it didn't die down until almost four a.m.!'

'Would you – would you like to talk about it out in the hallway?' I stammered.

She slapped her serviette beside her half-empty plate. 'No, I'd like to talk about it right here! My husband is still ill, and it's outrageous that we should have been subjected to—'

'Excuse me.' Suddenly Kathy leaned over towards

Mrs Dumont's table. 'I think we're the culprits, and I'm really sorry. Linda here is getting married next week, you see, and—'

Mrs Dumont's eyes snapped. 'Well, that's really no excuse!' She whipped her attention back onto me. 'Now, you tell your aunt that I certainly won't expect to be charged for last night, and I think some sort of recompense on top of that would be appropriate . . .'

She went on and on. I just stood there taking it, completely frozen in place, thanking God that my back was to Vampira. Praying that she wouldn't recognize me from my hair.

And then, out of the corner of my eye, I saw her. She had a hand still pressed to her forehead, and was heading for the door, staggering slightly. It opened and closed. She was gone.

'Poor Sam, she's not doing well this morning,' someone laughed behind me.

My knees went limp. Mrs Dumont was still raging on, saying, 'And I'll of *course* be taking this up with the Tourist Board, and—'

'You know,' broke in Kathy, 'I think it's great the way you waited for Sadie to turn up before you made your complaint. I mean, you could have bothered that other, *adult* woman with it, and it's so considerate of you that you didn't.' Her eyes glinted.

Mrs Dumont's mouth snapped shut like Kathy had jerked a string. 'I—'

'Just food for thought,' said Kathy sweetly.

Career Opportunities

Breakfast was a doddle after that. I served the rest of the hen party, and then the Brochus, who came into the dining room just after Vampira left. Mrs Dumont was nowhere to be seen; she had made herself scarce after Kathy had shut her up. With any luck, she'd stay that way until she left.

Finally everyone had eaten, and Mrs Marcus and I did the dishes.

'Well!' Her face was flushed as she smiled at me. 'That was quite an experience . . . I don't think being a bed and breakfast proprietor is in my future, somehow.' She folded up the dish towel, draping it neatly over the counter. (So she obviously *could* do housework; she just didn't do it in her own house.)

'*You* seem to have an aptitude for it, though,' she went on. 'You might have even found a career for yourself. You certainly seem to enjoy it.'

I stared at her. Enjoy it? Was she mad?

Mrs Marcus picked up her keys. 'Right, well, I'm leaving now, if your aunt doesn't need anything else. Will she be OK by tomorrow, do you think?'

I nodded vehemently. 'It's probably just a twenty-four-hour thing. Thank you so much for helping.' She wasn't so bad, once she loosened up a bit. If you took her away from all those dusty books, she might even become human.

After she left, I changed into a pair of jeans. I thought I'd go to the beach for a while, and then into town to do the shopping – that would give Vampira lots and lots of time to leave. I grabbed my wallet, and started out the back door.

'Sadie?' called a voice from the front of the house.

I hesitated, my hand on the doorknob. Finally I turned and went back through our flat, slipping quietly through the lounge so that I wouldn't disturb the Brochus if they were still in their room.

Kathy stood in the front hallway, wearing a pair of sunglasses. 'I just wanted to say goodbye,' she said. 'Thanks for taking such good care of us while we were here.'

I blushed. 'Oh, that's OK . . . I'm sorry about Mrs Dumont.'

Kathy held up her hands, laughing. 'No, *we're* sorry! Listen, don't worry about paying us back for the extra room; you can use that to give to Miss Hoity-Toity.' She glanced upstairs. 'By the way, I think Sam's gone back to sleep up there. Is it OK if she has a little nap? She's a bit worse for wear this morning.'

'Um – sure, that's OK.' God – Vampira with a hangover, camped out in my house! I'd spend a long time at the beach, then, and not come near Grace's again until her car was gone.

We walked to the front door together. It was a gorgeous blue day, with the boats in the bay looking

169

like they were on fire from the sun. Kathy gave me a hug. 'Right, take care, Sadie . . . it's been nice meeting you.'

Warmth rushed through me. She was so nice! How could she be friends with *Vampira*?

'You, too.' I hugged her back – and then I stiffened as if a viper had just slithered down my back. A green car was pulling up in our drive, and the driver was a woman with short, iron-grey hair.

No. No. Oh, my God.

It was Tricia.

The Wrong Direction

I stood frozen as Kathy opened the driver's door to her car and got in. With a friendly wave, she started up the engine and pulled off, her tyres rumbling over the gravel. *No, please don't go! Quick, chase after her, hang onto the door until she stops and lets you in—*

'Hello, Sadie.' Tricia was getting out of her car.

I swallowed against a dry throat. 'Hi.'

Her sandals crunched as she walked up the hill. 'Listen, I hope you don't mind my dropping by, but I saw Celia again yesterday, and she's really very worried about Leona . . . so I thought I'd just pop by and say hello to her, and then I can report back to Celia that everything's OK.'

'Oh, you've just missed her! That was her who just drove off.' My hands were trembling, but my voice came out totally natural. Sort of a mix of, *Oh, isn't this funny* and *Damn, I'm really sorry about that.*

Tricia stood in the sunshine a few paces away, watching me. 'That's a shame. Will she be gone for long?'

I gripped the edge of the door, longing to slam it shut and throw all the locks on. 'All day, I think. She had to go to Dartmouth for a— a dentist's appointment.'

Tricia peered up the road. 'She was going in the wrong direction, then.'

I swallowed. 'Oh – I think she was going by the shops first.'

Tricia let out a breath. 'Sadie, you saw me drive up, and you must have known why I was here. Why didn't you tell Leona to wait for a few minutes?'

My face was scorching, sizzling. 'I think she's already late—'

'Then why is she going by the shops?'

Thud. Dead pause.

Tricia climbed the steps until she was standing right in front of me. Inanely, I noticed that she stood a few inches taller than me, with strong, swimmer's shoulders. Her voice was gentle as she said, 'Sadie, I'm here to help. If anything's wrong, you can tell me.'

Yes, right, and what will happen if I do? My voice shook. 'Look, I don't know why she was heading in the wrong direction, but that was my Aunt Leona. OK?

Do you want, like, a signed statement or something?'

Her blue eyes met mine steadily. 'No, but I'd like to see someone who vaguely matches the description that your mother gave me.'

'She's – she's had a haircut—'

'*Sadie*. Stop it!' She gripped my shoulders and gave me a little shake, her eyes piercing into mine. 'Now, please tell me what is wrong! Is your aunt staying here with you?'

'Yes!'

'May I see her, then?'

'No – she's gone to Dartmouth, I told you.'

'Sadie, you're a bright girl – you must understand how important it is that I find out what's going on! Your mum is extremely worried. Now, for the last time, is your aunt here or not?'

'I've been wondering about that, too,' said a voice behind us.

I spun round, shaking. Vampira stood in the hallway with her bag over her shoulder, looking even paler than usual. I couldn't tell if it was the hangover, or what she had overheard.

She looked at Tricia, and managed a smile. 'I'm Sam Bodley, Sadie's Form Head . . . and I feel extremely stupid, but I stayed here with a party last night and didn't know it was Sadie's house. We've been worried about her at school for weeks now—'

Tricia nudged me aside in the doorway, coming in without even asking me. 'I'm Tricia McNair,' she said to Vampira, offering her hand. 'I'm a GBS volunteer who's been working with Sadie's mum at the hospital. Sadie's Aunt Leona hasn't been to the hospital to see her in over two weeks, and Celia is getting frantic that something is wrong.'

They both turned to look at me. 'Everything's fine!' I cried. 'She's just *out*, that's all. There's really no big deal.'

Vampira and Tricia glanced at each other. 'Sadie, why don't we sit down for a bit and have a chat?' said Vampira finally.

That's Her Now

They took over the lounge, sitting me down on the sofa and flanking me on either side like the Gestapo. I glanced at the door to Mum's room, praying that the Brochus were gone for the day.

'Now, Sadie, is your aunt actually here?' asked Vampira.

'No, she's gone to Dartmouth.' I bit a nail. It felt like my vital organs had turned to icy slush.

Her dark eyes flashed at me. 'I mean, *has* she been here? Since your mum went into hospital.'

'Of course! You don't think she'd just go off and leave me, do you?' I forced a laugh. Neither of them smiled.

'Why hasn't she been to see Celia, then?' demanded

Tricia. Her lined face looked very tanned against her grey hair.

'She's – just been angry. She wanted to go on holiday, you see, and then when Mum got ill she had to stay here. But she rang Mum at the hospital, I know she rang—'

Tricia's wide mouth twisted to one side. 'Yes, once I mentioned coming here, there was a phone message left. From someone claiming to be Leona.'

'It *was* my Aunt Leona!'

'That's interesting,' said Vampira dryly, drumming her red nails on the faded arm of the sofa. 'We've had a lot of phone calls from Leona at school, too. And from what I hear, Sadie's a dab hand at doing voices.'

My face burst into flames. *How* did she know that? 'That wasn't me! My aunt really did ring!'

Vampira shook her head, watching me. 'And what about that note that mysteriously appeared in Reception yesterday, saying you were in Scotland? You're never claiming your aunt wrote that!'

My pulse thudded in my ears. 'I— I only did it because Aunt Leona said she wasn't going to go to the meeting, and I didn't want her to get in trouble—'

'*Sadie.*' Tricia scraped her fingers through her hair. 'You're not telling us the truth, are you? We're trying to help, but you have to be honest with us!'

I spun towards her on the sofa. 'I am! Aunt Leona just doesn't like running the B&B, that's all, so I've had to help her out – doing breakfasts, and making

174

up the rooms and that. She's *here*, she just needs lots of help.'

Vampira gave me a narrow look. 'And that's why you've been late to school so often?'

'Yes! It's no big deal – I mean, I'm sorry I was late, but I had to help out, that's all—'

'But *why* hasn't Leona been to see Celia?' Tricia broke in. 'She must know how worried Celia would be – if she's here at all, there's no excuse for it.'

'Well, that's not my fault! She's always like that!' My voice sounded shrill, close to tears.

Tricia shook her head. 'No one's saying it's your fault, Sadie. But where is she?'

'I've told you! She's just gone for the day, but she'll be back—'

Vampira's lips pressed together. 'Sadie, I'm sorry, but I really don't believe you. Now—'

Suddenly, the front door slammed. 'Sadie!' called a voice.

I jerked upright as Vampira and Tricia looked at each other. And relief flooded through me. It felt like crawling through the scorching desert for a month, and then diving into a deep, endless pool.

'Sadie, are you here?' called the voice again.

I let out a breath, and smiled weakly at Tricia. 'In fact, that's . . . that's her now.'

Do Pardon Us

I went out into the front hallway, with Vampira and Tricia right behind me. Aunt Leona was just dragging her bags in. 'Oh, Sadie, I'm so glad to see you!' She scooped me up into a hug, her long hair tickling my neck. 'It's been such a nightmare, but I finally managed to switch the—'

'Aunt Leona, this is Tricia, the *GBS volunteer* who's been helping out with Mum,' I interrupted loudly. 'And Va— Miss Bodley, my form head.'

Aunt Leona's thin arms fell away from me. Her tanned cheeks reddened. 'Oh! I— um, nice to meet you.'

She leaned across her bags and held her hand out to Tricia, who paused a moment before shaking it. 'You're Leona?'

'Yes, that's me.' Aunt Leona smiled nervously.

'Leona, we've been very concerned about Sadie.' Vampira was leaning against the doorpost of our flat, arms crossed over her chest. 'Have you been staying here with her for the last two weeks?'

Aunt Leona looked quickly at me. 'Yes, of course. I mean, God, I wouldn't leave her on her own.'

'Why haven't you been to see Celia, then?' demanded Tricia.

Aunt Leona's face was phone-box red. 'I was – just

176

being stupid. I'll go this afternoon, and apologize to her.'

'And what about the meeting at school you were supposed to attend?' Vampira's eyes were narrowed into slits, the look I knew so well.

'I told you, she just didn't want to go to it,' I jumped in.

Vampira slid me a glance. 'I'd actually like to hear what Leona has to say.'

Aunt Leona licked her lips. 'I— well, I didn't want to go, like Sadie said. I'm sure she explained it all to you. I've just been really busy here, that's all.'

'You're carrying suitcases, though,' pointed out Tricia dryly.

My ribs tightened in my chest. 'Because she had to go back to London to pick up some clothes!' I blurted out. 'But she was only gone overnight, and there was a neighbour here to cook the breakfasts this morning. Right, Aunt Leona?'

'That's right.' Aunt Leona grabbed at a strand of hair, twisting it. 'I— I didn't know I'd have to stay here all summer when Celia took ill, you see, so I needed some of my things. I'm sorry, I know I shouldn't have left Sadie on her own last night. I'll be right here for the rest of the summer.'

Tricia and Vampira looked at each other.

The seconds ticked slowly by, and my knees went weak as I realized that we had got away with it. We had actually done it. Because even though I could tell from their faces that they didn't believe us, they couldn't *prove* anything. Tricia would have to leave now and report to Mum that Leona was here and all was well, and Vampira would slink back to her crypt, or wherever it was she lived.

Finally Tricia let out a short breath, shaking her silvery head. 'Well, it was very irresponsible of you, Leona, even if it was just for the one night—'

She broke off as the door to our flat creaked behind us. Everyone turned as Mr and Mrs Brochu came out into the hallway.

'Oh – do pardon us,' said Mrs Brochu, blinking. 'We're just going out for the day.'

Complete silence fell over us as they made their way to the front door, smiling tentatively, like they hoped maybe it would help to ward off all these loonies. 'I'm afraid we don't seem to have a key for the room,' said Mr Brochu to me.

My neck caught fire. 'No, I'm sorry . . . there isn't one.'

'Our things will be all right, though?' Mrs Brochu clutched her handbag, peering at me.

I nodded. I could feel everyone staring at me.

The Brochus left, walking up the road arm in arm like a pair of white-haired dolls. Everyone turned to look at me. Finally Vampira said, 'Sadie . . . how many bedrooms are in the flat?'

'Just – just two. But—'

'You rented out Celia's room?' Aunt Leona looked stricken.

I spun on her. 'I had to! But it was just for one

night – I mean, I knew you were gone for *only one night*, so—'

'But they don't seem to be leaving just yet, do they?' Vampira crossed her arms over her chest. 'Shall I go after them and ask how long they're staying here for?'

'No!' Tears choked my voice. 'No, please – it's not what you think—'

Tricia turned to Aunt Leona, her voice steely. 'Well now, Leona. It's obvious that you've been gone for a while, isn't it? And that Sadie wasn't expecting you back today. So do you want to tell us where you've been?'

Aunt Leona's face was sickly pale under her tan. Her lips trembled. 'The – the Canaries,' she whispered.

Tricia's mouth fell open. 'The *Canaries*?'

'Yes, but it was a mistake! I didn't mean to, I—'

'Wait a minute.' broke in Vampira. 'If you've been gone, then who—' She looked at me. 'Sadie, who's been running the B & B?'

'Me,' I mumbled.

Her eyes widened. She and Tricia stared at me, not saying anything.

'That's – that's why I've been late so often, and . . .' I trailed off.

Vampira shook her head briskly, like she was trying to wake herself up, and turned back to Aunt Leona.

'So you went off on holiday and left Sadie alone, is that it?' she said. 'A fourteen-year-old girl. You left her on her own to *run her mother's business.*'

'It's OK; she didn't mean to!' I flung out wildly.

179

'Please, don't tell anyone—'

Vampira had never looked so pale, so deadly calm. 'What, she didn't mean to fly off on a plane? Well, it's a pretty criminal mistake to make, and I think the police will be interested to hear about it.'

'No!' I lunged towards her and grabbed her arm. Hot, salty tears started down my face. 'You can't! You can't go to the police! I'll be taken into care – they'll tell my mum – please, you can't, it'll make her worse . . .'

They were all looking at me. I turned away, clutching my face and trying to hold in the sobs. It didn't work.

For a few minutes all I could hear was the sound of my own crying, echoing about the hallway. Then someone hugged me, holding me tightly, stroking my hair. 'Shh . . . it'll be OK . . .'

It was Vampira.

Tennis Match

Once I stopped crying – which probably only took a few minutes, but it felt like damp decades – Vampira let go of me and gave me a little pat.

'Are you all right now?'

'Yes,' I muttered, wiping my eyes. My face was in flames. I couldn't look at anyone.

'Let's go in and discuss this, then,' said Vampira.

It was an order, not a suggestion. 'We have some rather difficult decisions to make.'

Her voice was like ice shavings. Aunt Leona looked ill.

So for the second time that day we all sat in the lounge, with Tricia and Vampira beside me on the sofa again. Aunt Leona sat huddled in the armchair by the fireplace, looking like a prisoner about to be executed.

Tricia cleared her throat. 'The thing is, Sadie's right, you know.' She was sitting with her arm around my shoulders. I wasn't sobbing any more, but my stupid eyes kept leaking, like a tap that dripped in the night.

Vampira frowned, her long black hair almost blue against her pale skin. 'What do you mean?'

'Well, it may not actually make Celia *worse* to hear about Sadie being left on her own, but it would be an extremely stressful thing for her to hear in such a helpless state. Frankly, I think we should keep it from her if we can.'

Vampira didn't look thrilled at this. 'Yes, but Leona broke the law! We can't just shrug and pretend it never happened. She abandoned Sadie!'

'But I . . .' started Aunt Leona. She petered off as Vampira glared at her, shrinking back into her chair.

'I was OK.' I wiped my nose with a soggy tissue. My arms felt stiff, like I had been lifting weights at a gym.

Tricia's arm tightened around my shoulders. 'You were better than OK. You did an amazing thing, Sadie.'

Vampira's face softened, and she smiled at me. A real smile, open and human, and suddenly the thought of her being friends with Kathy wasn't so strange after all.

'Yes, I agree; Sadie's an amazing young woman. I don't know any other child in her year group who could have done what she did. You're really to be commended, Sadie.' Her eyes were warm with approval.

I blinked. Was this really Vampira, talking about *me*?

It only lasted a second, and then she was herself again. '*But*, it was still completely criminal of Leona to leave. And I don't see how we can just—'

'I agree, it was an awful thing to do,' broke in Tricia quietly. 'But now we have to do what's best for Celia, as well as for Sadie. And I really don't think that going to the police will help matters.'

Aunt Leona's eyes followed the conversation as if she were watching a tennis match. There was a pause while Vampira frowned, thinking it over. On the wall, the clock ticked softly.

Finally Aunt Leona swallowed. 'I – I'm really sorry. I won't do it again.'

Vampira snorted, and gave her a cold look. 'I know you won't, because I'm going to be checking up on you. And if you leave Sadie again, I'm going straight to the police, Celia or no Celia.'

The Full English, Take Two

The next morning I stood cooking at the hob, frying up eggs and flipping over the bacon that hissed on the grill. Aunt Leona worked at the counter behind me, hardly saying a word.

She had been very quiet ever since Vampira and Tricia had left the day before, moving her bags into my room without a murmur of protest. I had offered the Brochus one of the guest rooms upstairs when they got back from their stroll, but they had just smiled sweetly at me and said they were nicely settled in now, thank you. So Aunt Leona was sharing my room until they left.

Usually I hated sleeping with her – she snored like a chainsaw, and hogged all the covers – but I hadn't minded at all last night.

'Sadie – is this right?' said Aunt Leona suddenly. She showed me the mushrooms she was chopping. I glanced over my shoulder, scrambling eggs with a wooden spatula as I looked.

'Sure, that's fine. Maybe a bit smaller.'

'Smaller, right.' She frowned in concentration, carefully slicing the knife through each mushroom.

It was going to take her ages at that rate. I opened my mouth to say something – and then closed it again. It wouldn't be the end of the world if the mushrooms took a few minutes longer than usual.

'What?' Aunt Leona looked up suddenly, her face reddening.

'Nothing.' I flipped the hash browns over on the grill, and pricked the sausages with quick jabs of my knife. The tomatoes sizzled in the frying pan. 'I mean – thanks for helping.'

Aunt Leona looked confused for a moment, holding the knife like she had forgotten what to do with it. Then a small smile touched her face. 'That's OK. It's sort of the least I can do, don't you think?'

When the first lot of breakfasts were done, Aunt Leona took them into the dining room, carrying a plate in each hand and bumping backwards against the swinging door to open it. She was back a few minutes later, wrinkling her nose.

'Who's that woman out there? With the face like she just drank a pint of Dettol?'

I made a face, sliding fresh eggs onto a plate. 'Oh. Mrs Dumont. They're checking out tomorrow. Hopefully.'

Aunt Leona went back to slicing mushrooms, squinting down at the chopping board. 'She doesn't like you much, does she? Started going on about how rude you were, and how she wants a discount.'

Argh! 'Oh, I can't believe she's still going on about that—'

Aunt Leona shrugged her thin shoulders. 'Well, I told her to get over herself and leave, if she hated it so much here.'

My mouth dropped, imagining Mrs Dumont's face. Blimey, it must have been priceless. 'You didn't!'

My aunt grinned at me over her shoulder. 'Oh, I assure you I did. And I also told her to stop slagging off my niece, who, by the way, just happens to be the manageress.'

When the Living Is Easy

So for the rest of the summer, I ran the B&B. And I don't know if it was Marcus's website or what, but we were busier than we had ever been, with all the rooms filled almost every night. The weeks passed in a whirl of making breakfasts, talking to the guests, checking people in, cleaning – and smiling away like a mad thing. And then one day I realized that I hadn't had to remind myself to smile in ages; it was just there.

Aunt Leona helped with all of it. She still snapped at me sometimes if I butted in too much, and had her days when she was *soo* obviously not enjoying it at all . . . but slowly, slowly, she started to get the hang of it, so that by the time I had to go back to school she could just about do everything on her own. She even learned how to fold the swans.

When I had time to myself, I saw Milly sometimes. It turned out that we had loads of quirky stuff in common – like we had the same sense of humour, and both loved Johnny Depp movies. Not to mention that she liked tennis, so I dusted off my racket and we played a lot, sometimes sunbathing down at the beach afterwards. We could talk for hours, about pretty much anything. Or not say anything at all.

I visited Mum every day. We got really good at using something called an alphabet card, so that we could zap conversations back and forth almost like she was talking. We talked a lot about Dad that summer.

I also read that book of Marcus's – the *How to Run a Perfect B&B* book. Only Greg R. Smeed couldn't have been the big expert he claimed, because he didn't say anything I didn't already know. He kept going on about things that I had already been doing for weeks, like putting fresh flowers out in the entrance hallway, and keeping flyers of all the Brixham tourist attractions on the front table.

I mean, it wasn't rocket science.

Not a Hero

Our new English teacher was Mrs Sayle. During her first lesson, she had leaped about like an excited cricket, chirping on about stories and truth, and how she was going to take us on an odyssey of the mind that year. Which had impressed nobody, so she had taken the hint and calmed down a bit.

'Quick writing exercise,' she said now, pacing about in front of the room. 'I want you to describe a place that you know very well. Bring it to life for me, so that I can see it, feel it, *taste* it for myself. Right? Ten minutes, go!'

I bit my lip and opened up my orange exercise book, waiting for the absolute dread to hit my stomach, freezing my brain, paralysing my fingers.

But it didn't come. It felt so bizarre, like hanging about on a platform waiting for a train to arrive that had actually been cancelled and no one had told me. I hardly knew what to do with an exercise book in front of me and no panic.

Beside me, Milly already had her head down, her hand flying over the page. I glanced at her sideways, and could see her eyes shining; she loved stuff like this.

I looked down at the blank lined sheets. Well, I didn't love it. But . . . I felt like maybe I could do it.

I picked up my pen and started to write.

Afterwards we had break, and Milly and I fought our way through the corridors, heading out to the courtyard. I saw Hannah and Tara and the others over in our old spot, and I waved. I had sort of been dreading seeing them again when the new term started, but it had turned out to be no big deal. We just said hi when we saw each other in the corridors, and that was that.

'You know what's strange?' said Milly as we leaned against the wall.

'No, what?'

'Well—' She rummaged in her bag, taking out a pack of crisps. 'It's the way that no one knows what you did last term. I mean, you should be this complete celebrity, with people stopping you in the halls and begging on their knees for your autograph, but . . . nada. No one's got a clue.'

It was a grey day, with the clouds hanging down so low you could practically touch them. I took a Coke out of my bag and snapped it open, making a face at her.

'Why would anyone know? It wasn't in the papers or anything.'

Milly laughed, her grey eyes looking like part of the clouds. 'Yes, that's exactly what I like about you, Sadie . . . you really don't get it.'

'Get what?'

She popped a crisp in her mouth. 'Has it never occurred to you that anyone else would have told everyone? Would perhaps have bandied it about that they were, like, this complete hero—'

'You're barking! I'm not a hero!'

Milly grinned, shaking her head. 'OK,' she said. 'Not a hero. Whatever.'

Seeing Things

The nurses smiled at me as I walked down the corridor. 'Back in school, eh?' said Brenda, flicking my tie. She hadn't seen me in a couple of days.

'Yeah, Year Ten.'

She laughed. 'Oh dear, GCSE's . . .'

Which obviously I knew, since everyone kept going on about it. My stomach dipped, thinking about it. *No, stop it,* I told myself. *It won't be as bad as you think.*

I walked into Mum's room and stopped short. 'Your tube is gone!'

She sat up in bed, smiling at me. 'I wanted to surprise you,' she said.

'Mum! Oh, that's so great!' I rushed to her bed and hugged her, and for the first time in months, her arm was strong enough to wrap around me in return. I sank back onto her bed, grinning. 'You can really talk again!'

'Just about.' She put a hand to her bandaged throat and swallowed. 'It's a bit rough from the tube, but it's there.'

I started to say something else, and stopped as she touched my jacket, tugging at it playfully.

'Year Ten, eh?'

'Yeah. And Mum, I wanted to show you—'

'How did you do today?'

I stiffened. The world stood completely still as her words hung in the air like cigarette smoke. She looked at me expectantly, eyes gleaming, waiting to hear about perfect marks.

'Sadie?'

I stood up slowly. I was shaking. 'I'm – I'm not going to tell you.'

Her eyes widened. 'Sadie—'

'It's all you care about!'

'Sadie, that's not true—' She stopped, coughing.

'It *is* true! Every single day, that's all you ever talked about – how did you do, how did you do! The second you get your voice back, you're asking about it! The next thing will be my homework, won't it – going on like it's the end of the world! Well, it's not. And you know what? I can do well if I want to, if no one's breathing down my neck and quizzing me every second!' I fumbled with my rucksack, grabbed my English essay out of the folder. 'But I don't need to.'

I tore the essay up.

Mum's face looked like I had slapped her. 'Sadie . . .' she whispered. 'Oh, Sadie, I'm sorry.'

I didn't answer her. I stood staring down at the scattered scraps of paper. *B – good work!* was on one of them.

Mum swallowed. 'Please sit down. I can't talk very loud.'

I sat on the edge of the bed and looked away. Mum groped for my hand, tried to squeeze it. 'Oh, I'm so stupid,' she said. 'Sadie, I'm sorry; I just asked out of habit, out of stupid, *stupid* habit! Oh, love, you're absolutely right, and I knew it months ago.'

Tears sprang to my eyes. I held myself tightly, not letting it show.

She coughed again, wincing. 'You were lying to me about your marks last term, weren't you? You weren't really doing that well.'

My head snapped up. 'How did you . . .'

'I don't know. It was just something in your face, or your voice – it was like I noticed more when I couldn't talk.' Her eyes were moist. She wiped them with the back of her hand and tried to laugh. 'You know, GBS takes away absolutely everything, but one thing it does give you is a lot of time to think . . . and Sadie, I realized what I've been doing to you, putting you under so much pressure.'

I stared at her. 'But—'

'And I decided that I'd wait until I had my voice back to talk to you about it . . . and what do I do but put my foot in it the second I open my mouth!'

I looked at the raw place on her throat that the bandages didn't quite cover, and then away. I didn't know what to say.

Mum's voice came slowly, painfully. 'Sadie, I— well, I always wanted more for myself, you know. Felt that I should have a degree, that I was stupid because I didn't. I just wanted you to have an education you could be proud of . . . or at least I told myself it was for you, but I guess really . . .' She trailed off, and touched my arm. 'I'm sorry, Sadie. Please forgive me.'

I pulled away. 'Well— well what if I don't want to go to uni? Or even college? Because I've been thinking about it a lot, and I want to leave school when I turn sixteen.'

Her throat moved. 'I see.' There was a pause. 'What would you do?'

I plucked at her bedsheet. 'I don't know . . . maybe take a hotel apprenticeship somewhere, or even just work at Grace's. I've been – been helping out Aunt Leona a lot. I like it.'

I looked up, and saw the struggle caught on her face. And I thought, *Right, that's torn it, forget about being all understanding and sorry,* but then she nodded slowly.

'Well . . . fair enough. It's your life.' She saw my jaw drop to the floor, and smiled. 'Whatever you want to do is fine, Sadie. I've realized I couldn't be more proud of you, just the way you are.'

She touched my hair. 'Listen, let's – let's not lose what we found when I couldn't talk, OK? I want to stay your friend.'

'OK,' I said softly. I felt a smile grow through me, and then we were hugging each other tightly, sort of laughing and crying at the same time. Whatever it was, it felt good.

'And you know what else?' Mum said when we pulled apart.

'What?' I dabbed my eyes with the corner of her sheet.

She grazed my cheek with her fingers. 'I've realized how very much like Frank you are.'

I smiled down at her bed. My paper was still scattered all over the floor, and suddenly I was stooping down, gathering up the pieces. 'Mum, do you want to hear this?'

'If you want me to.'

'Yeah, it's – well, we were supposed to describe a place that we know really well, and – well, just listen.' I arranged the pieces on her bed, fitting them together like a paper jigsaw, and started to read.

The Intensive Care unit at Brixham Hospital has white shiny walls, and it's full of nurses rushing about, pushing carts and carrying clipboards with important papers on them. It smells like antiseptic, so clean that it hurts, and you can hear TVs going and sometimes the nurses shouting something when there's an emergency.

My mother's room is there, in IC as they call it. I see other rooms as I walk down the corridors on my way to hers, and they all look the same, with white walls and a TV and beds with metal railings on them.

But my mother's room is different, because she's in it. I sit on her clean white bed with her, and we talk even though she can't speak. There are always flowers on her table that Tricia brings from her shop, usually things like carnations, but sometimes lilies that open up and scent the whole room. The walls are just plain white like the others, with a TV hanging on them, but somehow it all looks friendlier in here.

But the main thing I see in Mum's room is her eyes. They are milk-chocolate brown with soft hazel flecks that catch the light, which I never noticed before she came into hospital and we spent so much time looking at each other.

I'm very glad that I've seen my mother's eyes now, and know exactly what they look like, so that I can shut my own eyes and see them whenever I want to.

I stopped, and looked at her from under my hair. 'That's um . . . that's all. She gave me a B on it; she said she had to take something off for my spelling.'

Mum swallowed. 'Oh, Sadie . . .' She reached for my hand, gripped it as hard as she could. 'Thank you,' she whispered.

It's Also on Powerpoint

I hummed to myself as I rearranged the photos on the end tables, adjusting them so that they made perfect angles. Dad smiled at me from one of them, holding up his paintbrush like a salute – that was the day he and Mum had got into a paint fight as he was doing up one of the rooms. I smiled back, remembering, and then turned away and dusted the table until it gleamed. There was no reason to, really – Aunt Leona and I had cleaned everything the day before, before she went back to London – but I liked seeing the wood shine.

Mum sat at the dining table, going through the mountain of post that had piled up over the summer. Her hands still shook slightly as she slit the envelopes open, but Dr Sarjeem had said that would fade away over the next few weeks.

'And then you'll be back to your old self again,' he had said, smiling at her. Mum had winked at me when he said it. 'Well, maybe not quite,' she said.

Suddenly she jerked up straight in her chair, as though cement had been poured down her spine. 'Why – what on earth—?'

I looked up. 'What?'

Her brown hair had grown longer in hospital, and it fluffed about her face, making her cheekbones look softer. She shook her head, staring at a sheet of paper. 'There's been some mistake, there must have been! This can't be my bank balance!'

I put my cloth down and went over and looked. The list of deposits marched down the sheet, regular as breakfast. The total was . . . a lot, actually. My eyes widened as I stared at it.

Mum twisted in her chair to look up at me. 'Sadie, is this right? How much has Leona been putting in, do you know?'

'Um . . .' I looked down at the sheet, trying to work out all the figures. 'We were really busy all summer; we made deposits a few times a week. I never really checked how much was in there . . .' I trailed off.

Mum flipped through the sheets. 'Four hundred

and seven pounds deposited on September thirtieth
. . . three hundred and sixty pounds on the twenty-
seventh . . . usually I don't have anything left after the
direct debits for the bills have gone out!'

'Those sound right,' I said faintly. Had they really
added up to that much?

Both of us jumped as the back door opened and
closed. A second later Marcus came into the room,
holding a blue plastic folder. A lock of his brown hair
stuck up in the back like he had gelled it, only being
Marcus, he probably didn't even know that gel existed.

'Hi, Mrs Pollock. My mum told me you were home
from hospital,' he said cheerfully.

'Oh, hello, Marcus.' Mum frowned back down at
the statement, running a finger down the rows of figures.

He wiped his glasses on the front of his white shirt,
and shot me a look. 'See, Sadie? I *told* you that
statistically, the odds were in her favour. Appliance of
science. You should be more logical, instead of getting
all upset.'

My face burned with irritation. 'I didn't hear you
knock, Marcus.'

He squinted at me, and hooked his glasses back
on. 'Why would I knock? Anyway, it's your mum I've
come to see. I thought she'd like to see my business
analysis of Grace's.' He held up the folder.

'A— your what?' Mum blinked, looking up.

'I've also got it on Powerpoint, if you'd like a
presentation.' He pulled a CD out of the folder. It
glinted like liquid silver.

Dad Would Approve

A few minutes later the three of us were clustered around the computer as Marcus flipped through multi-coloured slides. 'OK, this picture of the sad, skinny house represents the year before you went into hospital. Look at the graph – do you see how business is so sporadic here? Your bank balance stays reasonably constant, but after your outgoings, you—'

'*Hang* on,' interrupted Mum, looking stunned. 'How did you get my bank balance?'

'I looked in your accounts folder on the PC, of course.' Marcus clicked the mouse, and the picture changed. 'Right, so here the house is looking more cheerful. This is the two-week period just after you went into hospital, when it was just Sadie and me on our own. We implemented several changes immediately, starting with—'

'What?' Mum's eyes bulged.

The ocean roared through my head, knocking me off my feet. My hands clenched as I stared at Marcus's moronic picture of the happier house. I couldn't look at Mum.

'We implemented—'

'What do you mean, just Sadie and you on your own? Where was Leona?'

'Well, she'd left—' Marcus stopped, his face ripening. 'Um . . .'

Mum whipped about in her seat and stared at me. '*Sadie?* Where was Leona? What does he mean, she left?'

My throat had gravel in it. 'She . . . she went to the Canaries,' I whispered.

Mum slumped back in her chair. No one said anything for a moment. The computer hummed to itself.

'I knew it,' said Mum finally. 'I didn't want to know it, but I knew it anyway . . .'

Marcus cleared his throat. 'OK, um, moving on . . . now we have a picture of a fat, happy house. This is after the website went live, once—'

Mum pushed her chair back and stood up. 'Marcus,' she said gently. 'Go home. Come back in an hour or so. We'll look at your presentation then.'

'Oh. OK.' Marcus saved the presentation and logged off, moving the mouse about the mat. 'It's not completely finished anyway. I must be overlooking something in the figures – your business has got loads better, but I know it can't all be down to the website, because only around fifteen per cent of bookings come from that. I'm still trying to figure it out.' His glasses furrowed onto his nose as he frowned.

'See you soon, Marcus,' prompted Mum.

'Bye, Mrs Pollock. Bye, Sadie.' He hopped off the chair, picking up his folder.

Mum looked at me after the door closed, her

expression flat. 'What happened, then?'

So I told her.

It took ages, and at the end I sat in my chair, frozen, waiting for the explosion. But she just stood there looking dazed, her face a complete blank. I cleared my throat. 'Mum, we didn't tell you because you were so ill – we didn't want you to worry—'

'I just can't believe that Leona did that,' whispered Mum. 'She *left* you, all on your own—'

'Oh, it was OK,' I said awkwardly. 'I mean, it was sort of hard to keep everything going and not get caught, but—'

I broke off as she pulled me up into a bone-breaking hug. 'Oh, Sadie, don't say a word. Just—I'm so proud of you, you know that?' Suddenly her voice sounded scratchy again, like the first day without her tube.

Tears filled my eyes. I hugged her back, not saying anything. Through the open window, I could hear seagulls, and the faint murmur of the bay. I held onto Mum tightly as the soft scent of her apple shampoo wrapped around me.

Finally we let each other go. Both of our faces were damp, and we burst out laughing as we looked at each other.

'What a pair, eh,' Mum blew her nose.

I wiped my eyes and nodded. 'Pathetic. Like a pair of leaky taps.' She dabbed at her nose again. 'You know what?' she said. 'I've been thinking that Marcus might need to do a bit more work on that brilliant website of his.'

I blinked, wondering what Marcus's website had to do with anything. 'But – he says he's got it all fixed.'

Mum put on a musing expression, resting a finger on her chin and looking around the room. 'Yes, I know, but I was thinking that it might be about time for a change. I mean, Grace's Place . . . it's sort of an old-fashioned name, don't you think?'

I clutched her arm. '*Mum!* You can't change the name! It's what Dad named it—'

'Oh, I think he'd approve of this, actually.' Mum smiled at me, tucking a strand of hair behind my ear. 'I think it would be nice to call it Sadie's Place.'